THE SURGEON'S
BABY SECRET.

BY
AMBER McKENZIE

MILLS &
BOON

Published in Great Britain 2015
by Mills & Boon, an imprint of Harlequin (UK) Limited,
Eton House, 18-24 Paradise Road, Richmond, Surrey, TW9 1SR

ISBN: 978-0-263-24690-2

To all my female physician friends. Heather, Kate, Jaclyn, KP, Erin, Allison, Rebecca and Kristen, it has been amazing being your friend and colleague. Thank you for sharing your lives and friendship with me. You are all both talented and beautiful, like the perfect romance novel heroine.

CHAPTER ONE

WAS SHE RUNNING away from her problems? Yes—and who could blame her? Erin thought as she ventured farther up the hills that comprised Arthur's Seat. Was it working? No. Her trip across the Atlantic to Edinburgh had done nothing to change her circumstances or block the thoughts and feelings that had been tormenting her. The message that had awaited her at hotel check-in had confirmed that.

She looked around her at the lush greenery of the hills, the blue of the sky and the distant sparkle of the ocean. It was breathtaking, even with the signs warning of the dangers of severe wind gusts. She wished everything in life could come with such warnings. Then maybe she would have seen the hidden danger that had been disguised as her dreams coming true.

Erin stopped to catch her breath and smiled ruefully to herself. She felt as if she spent every day running from one delivery to another as an obstetrics resident, but maybe she wasn't as fit as she'd thought, as she took in another deep breath. She looked up the path and saw a bench and made her way toward it. Maybe this hadn't been her best idea. She hadn't even dressed for a hike, her gray blazer and heeled boots a poor choice for any athletic pursuit. But this hadn't been her plan. Nothing had been her plan. But another message from her now ex-husband had pushed her into the open air before she had even set sight on her hotel room.

She felt another wave of anger pass through her just as another gust of cold wind hit. She wanted to still be angry with him. Anger, indignation, hurt, she had felt them all when the truth had first come out, but now all those emotions she had once felt toward Kevin Dufour, her newly ex-husband, had long ago burnt out and had been replaced by disappointment in herself.

She reached back into the pocket of her blazer and pulled out the printed message that had interrupted her attempt at escape.

Erin—Divorce finalized. I think we can agree that you don't belong at Boston General. Kevin

Was he right? Was it worth having to deal with the aftermath of Kevin to stay where she loved to work? Damn, she was doing it again, letting someone else make her doubt herself. Why was she so weak? How had she been so naive?

She felt the gust as she watched the note slip from her hands and tumble down the slope. Instinctively she lunged for it, not wanting Kevin's cruel words to sully the beauty of the landscape surrounding her.

He watched, as if in slow motion, as the woman jumped from the steep hilltop over the edge. For a split second he froze before he sprinted to the spot where he'd last seen her. In the short time before he got there he prepared himself for what he might find and felt relief at the sight of her holding onto the last small outcropping of rock before the hill's cliff. He couldn't make out much of her face as she hugged her body close to the almost vertical ground beneath it, but he saw her tremble with fear. "Don't move," he yelled down to her.

But she did move, her head tilted only slightly to look back up at him, and once again he felt shock at what he was seeing. She was both young and beautiful. Her shoulder-length dark blond hair was being flung around her face as the wind continued to battle with her. Through the wisps of hair he could make out the beautiful large eyes that stood out even more against the pallor of her complexion. He was sure that he would never forget the way this woman was looking at him right now, at this moment.

"Stay still," he reminded her, not wanting to be a distraction to her.

"I'm scared," a small voice came back to him.

He wasn't surprised. Even though he had watched her willingly throw herself from the hilltop it was normal to have last-minute regrets. He needed to keep her calm and establish trust between them. "I know. I'm going to get you out of there. What's your name?"

"Erin."

"Okay, Erin. My name is Ryan and I'm going to help you."

How could he appear so calm and confident? She was literally on a ledge, facing death. Just as she had been reaching for the message a large gust of wind had blown it—and her—over the cliff. If she had thought she had hit rock bottom before, she had been wrong. This was truly it. She had let Kevin's words literally drive her over the edge, and for what? What did it matter? What did he matter? Nothing that had come before this moment mattered except she had never wanted a second chance more than she wanted one now.

She looked up again toward the reassuring voice from above. The sun was shining brightly and she was too afraid to move any further, so all she could take in was the man's muscular silhouetted outline. It immediately instilled confidence in her and she felt some of her fear dissipate. If anyone could help her it was this man.

She watched as he lowered himself to the ground, lying prone, hanging his head and shoulders over the cliff's edge. He extended one long muscular arm toward her. "Erin, when you are ready I want you to reach up and take my hand."

"I can't." The idea of letting go of any of her grip on the limited ground beneath her was impossible.

"Yes, you can, Erin. Trust me."

It was an even more impossible request. She didn't trust anyone, not even herself. "I can't."

"You can't stay where you are forever. Reach up and take my hand."

He was right. She had no options. Still, she couldn't help but marvel at the complete lack of frustration in his voice. When was the last time someone had been patient with her? Or even acknowledged her feelings? Trust? She had sworn against that. But right now she had little more to lose so she took a deep breath and reached out her hand. The moment her arm was fully extended she felt his hand pass hers and grip strongly around her wrist; instinctively she did the same. Then, as if she weighed nothing, she was being lifted until he could grasp her under her shoulders and they both went tumbling toward the ground.

But instead of the ground, she landed on him and felt herself being raised and lowered with his breath, her body lax against his firmness. She was too dazed to move as she took in everything that had just happened. He had saved her, this man, Ryan. Ryan, who appeared to have Herculean strength. Ryan, who smelled like a combination of sunshine and sweat. Ryan, whose whole body she was in contact with.

She rolled herself to his side and for the first time got a good look at the man who had saved her. He was more impressive up close. He was tall and there was no muscle on his body that wasn't defined. His black tech running shirt and blue shorts showed off the golden bronze of his skin. His hair was a light brown and he had a scar that extended from above his deep blue eyes toward his thick cropped hair. She could see at least one tattoo revealing itself from the short sleeve of his left arm.

"Are you okay?" His voice cut through her mental inventory of his assets.

Was she? No, but that wasn't what she wanted to say and likely not what her hero wanted to hear. "Yes."

"Are you disappointed?" he asked, his voice softer than before.

Disappointed? Had he sensed her evaluation? Truth be told, he was the first man she had felt attracted to in over a year and his raw sex appeal and heroism left little room for disappointment.

"No," she answered, embarrassed.

"Good," he replied, appearing relieved. He deftly sprang to his feet and then reached out a hand, which she took, and he helped her do the same. He was tall, her head coming up only to the top of his shoulders as she had to tilt upward to look at him.

"Thank you. I don't know what I would have done if you hadn't saved me." She heard her voice tremble at the end, the direness of her previous circumstance even more apparent now that she was out of it.

"I'm just happy you wanted to be saved. Now, let's get out of here before the wind picks up."

She was shocked when he reached out to take her hand. So shocked that she didn't pull away, not that she could have even if she had wanted to. His grip was as tight as it had been when he had pulled her up. It was as if he was locking her beside him and didn't want her to get away. She should have felt fear. This man, Ryan, was a stranger, but instead she felt taken care of. It was a feeling she hadn't felt in a very long time and she was in no hurry to lose it. So instead she followed his lead and walked with him toward the base of the hillside.

"You're American." He finally broke their silence after several minutes.

"Yes." And she realized from his accent that he must be, too.

"What brings you to Scotland?"

"I'm running away from the disaster my life has become. You?" She almost gasped as she realized the answer that had run through her mind at high speed had also escaped from her mouth.

"Work." He answered as though her response had been completely normal and she welcomed his tact.

"What do you do?"

"I'm in the military."

"That explains it." She covered her mouth with her free hand. What was wrong with her? What was it about this man that made her lose her ability to filter? She turned her focus from the path ahead to look at him and was met with a similar appraisal.

"Explains what?" He had stopped and she felt his blue eyes question her more strongly than his words had.

"I just meant that…" Was it that he was the only man with scars and a tattoo that she had ever found sexy? Or that his bravery and strength in saving her had seemed so effortless it wasn't surprising he was a professional hero?

"It's okay, you don't need to explain yourself." He began walking again and she followed, still linked with him. Time went by as they made their way toward the hill's base and she marveled at how comfortable the silence was between them.

"It's a beautiful country." His words finally broke through.

"Yes, it is," she agreed, more comfortable with the neutral territory their conversation had achieved.

"Have you ever been here before?"

"No, but I feel like I have. My father grew up here and when I was little he would tell me stories from his childhood or sometimes just about this faraway country with princess castles and green grass and blue ocean as far as the eye could see."

"I'm not sure the Scottish would take well to having a strong part of their heritage referred to as 'princess castles.'" She looked back toward him and he was smiling. If she had thought he was handsome before, now he was devastating. She was shocked by the powerful wave of attraction his smile evoked and had to check herself against those feelings. Fortunately they had reached the end of the path, a natural place to say goodbye. She let go of his hand and was surprised by the feeling of loss. All the more reason to get away now before she let her attraction make her life more complicated.

"Thank you again."

"I'll walk you back to your hotel."

She wanted him to, but knew better. "Thanks. But I'm okay from here. I can find my way."

She knew he was going to argue with her so she didn't give him the chance. Instead she turned and headed toward her hotel and never looked back at the kindest, most handsome man she had talked to in years.

She looked nothing like Sabrina but she reminded him of her nonetheless. Both women were beautiful, but that wasn't the similarity that was troubling him. It was the look in her eyes that brought back familiar haunting memories. At first those large round eyes that he'd later learned were a deep blue had just seemed scared, but after she had been returned to safety their depth of emotion had changed from fear to sadness. A sadness he had seen in his sister Sabrina's eyes years ago and which had set off warning bells in his head—not that she hadn't already rung those bells hard by leaping off the hill's edge. What would she have done if he hadn't been there? Would she have followed through with her intention and let go?

He physically recoiled at the thought of losing her and stopped in his tracks. How could he already feel a connection to this woman he barely knew? Most people would blame the dramatic nature of their encounter, but truthfully, to him, that drama had been minor. He was a military trained physician and for the past five years had had a decorated career as a trauma specialist. Pulling a beautiful woman to safety was a nice day at the office compared to the horrors he had witnessed.

It must be the emotional resemblance to Sabrina. The first time he'd seen that look in Sabrina he had missed it. He had been away for too long and hadn't noticed the sadness in his little sister's eyes. His role as a big brother had circumvented his role as a physician and he'd missed all the warning signs of depression his sister had been experiencing. She had been thinner than he'd remembered, with dark rings of fatigue under her eyes. She had rarely smiled and when he had tried to arrange activities to cheer her up, she had gotten no pleasure out of things that had previously made her happy.

Classic depression, and he, her big brother, the physician, had missed it and had just thought she'd been heartbroken and would get over it. That she had been better off. But in the end that hadn't mattered. Instead, Sabrina had suffered for over a year before she'd hit rock bottom and he had never stopped blaming himself. He should have been there for her. He should have recognized the signs and gotten help for her earlier. He had failed her. He hadn't protected her from the man who had broken her heart and he hadn't realized how badly she'd needed help to be put back together.

The thought monologue snapped him back to Erin. She had thanked him for saving her. He wished that it was enough to reassure him. Hadn't Sabrina always smiled politely through her pain? The one thing he was certain of was that this was not their last encounter. Was it a sense of responsibility he felt to her? Intrigue at the cause of her sadness? Or the fact that she smelled of wildflowers and had felt soft and right pressed against him. At this point it didn't matter, his mind was made up. This was not the end of their story, it was merely the beginning.

CHAPTER TWO

ERIN SPOONED ANOTHER morsel of the warm decadent bread pudding into her mouth and let both the food and the ambiance overwhelm her senses. The local pub she had ventured to for dinner had been everything she'd been looking for; the noise and activity were a perfect distraction from the constant replay of her own thoughts. She had almost died today. She might have died had Ryan not saved her. The worst part was it would have been a stupid reason to die.

She needed to take responsibility for inadvertent actions. For her constant ability to let people, mainly her now ex-husband, manipulate her. But today it stopped. When she'd got back to her hotel room, she had torn up the new messages that awaited her and instead lounged in a hot bath and thought about what she wanted in life. She wanted to make a difference to the lives of others, just as Ryan had done for her today. The best way to do that was through her work as an obstetrician-gynecologist. So there was no way she was going to leave her training at Boston General, no matter what demands her ex made.

"Is this seat taken?" A deep voice interrupted her repetition of the earlier inner pep talk. She looked up and saw Ryan. He had changed from his running clothes and was flawless in a button-down navy collared shirt and charcoal-gray dark denim. How was it possible in a city of five hundred thousand people she would run into Ryan again? Attraction followed by fear coursed through her. She wanted to say yes and protect herself from once again being swayed by a handsome man, but how could she? Ryan had saved her life. The least she could do was agree to let him join her table.

"No, go ahead," she agreed, gesturing to the single chair opposite her.

"Are you staying nearby?"

"Yes. You?"

"At the Glasshouse." She felt her eyebrows rise and her eyes widen as he named her hotel. It felt as if they were being drawn together and that was a tough feeling to reconcile in the face of her newfound decision to take charge of her own life.

"How long are you going to be in Edinburgh?" Maybe he would be gone before she had to worry about her feelings toward him.

"A few days. You?"

"The same." Of course, she thought to herself. She took a long sip of the local rhubarb cider she had nursed throughout her meal.

"So you are not running away from your life permanently?"

She looked up to meet his eyes, surprised that he had raised her impulsive comment. "No, I'm afraid that is not an option."

"Glad to hear it." The waitress arrived at their table and took Ryan's order. She was a gorgeous Scottish redhead, tall with a body as luxurious as her hair. She waited for Ryan to notice but he was polite and otherwise unconcerned with the other woman. "I hope you don't mind sticking around for a bit. It's been a long time since I've had good company."

"How do you know I'll be good company?"

"Because you're beautiful to look at and you speak your mind, making you interesting to talk to. It's a rare but highly sought-after combination."

He thought she was beautiful. When had she last heard that? She tucked a lock of her hair behind her ear before finally looking up to meet his eyes. "I don't know what to say to that."

"You don't have to say anything, Erin. That's the benefit of having dinner with a stranger. You don't owe me anything."

"I think I owe you a lot," she acknowledged.

"So tell me something about yourself and we'll call it even."

She thought of all the things she could tell him. She was a physician. She worked at the same hospital as her stepfather and ex-husband. She was recently divorced from the only man she had ever been in a serious relationship with. None of those topics she wanted to discuss. "I was born in Scotland."

"You don't sound Scottish." He was smiling at her and she couldn't help but feel a sense of warmth from him.

"We moved when I was one. This is my first time back."

"Your father never brought you here when you were growing up?"

"No. My father died when I was ten."

He reached across the table and rested his hand on hers. "I'm sorry."

This was where she normally said "That's okay" as casually as she could muster, but something about Ryan changed her response. "Thank you."

His hand lingered on hers until the waitress returned with his dark draft beer. "So tell me something about yourself," she said, genuinely interested in the man before her.

"What do you want to know?"

"Am I the first woman you have ever pulled off a hillside?"

"First, and hopefully last. What else?" He leaned back in his chair and looked completely relaxed with opening his life up to her questions.

"Where are you stationed?"

"I've been mainly in combat zones in the Middle East for the past five years."

"Do you like it?"

"Combat?"

"Being in the military."

"Yes. I originally joined to help pay for school but found myself drawn to the hard work ethic and structure. When I finished school I decided to stay for the challenge."

"You like a challenge?" She was surprised to hear her own voice almost coy, teasing him.

"I've found that everything in life worth having you have to work for." The smile that followed was enough to make her heart begin to race. Was he flirting with her? A second later a horrible thought flashed through her mind and in a moment it also left her mouth.

"Are you married?" She alternated her gaze between the look in his eyes during his response and an examination of his left hand, looking for any hint of an outline of a ring.

"No, never have been." It seemed as if he was telling the truth, but would she know if he wasn't? He didn't seem at all disturbed by her question. "Are you?"

She thought about her new label, hating the way it made her relive all her mistakes every time the label was used. She took another sip of her cider and rested the glass back on the table before answering. "Divorced."

"That bothers you."

"You're observant," she acknowledged.

"I've built my career around paying attention to the subtle clues people give me."

"Then you're lucky. I'm so naive that I miss even the most obvious of signs people give me."

"You don't strike me as naive."

"I'm not anymore." Or that was her new resolve anyway. She still needed to prove it to herself.

"I get the feeling there is a story behind that."

He was more than observant, he was perceptive and he was right. There was a long story behind the loss of her innocence, but not one that she felt like sharing—especially with Ryan. It had been years since she had been a stranger to anyone and she enjoyed the freedom of talking to someone who wasn't privy to the backstory of her life. "Are you always this inquisitive with women you have barely met?"

"No. But considering how we met I think we're already beyond the superficial, don't you?"

It wasn't his words that implied an intimacy between them. It was the way he was looking at her. She again took in the man sitting before her. He was as handsome as he was confident and, as silly as it felt, it felt as if he was on her side. She wasn't sure which feature she found most attractive but attraction was definitely coursing through her body.

"Yes," she answered. "What exactly are we doing here, Ryan?"

She was direct. He'd known that already but he still wasn't prepared for her question, because he didn't know the answer. He had thought about little other than her since they had last parted. Relief had been just one of the emotions he had felt when he'd seen her tonight. If it had only been relief he would have just been happy to see that she was all right and left her alone, but more than relief he felt a complete fascination with the woman he had spotted the moment he'd entered the restaurant.

She looked more mature and somehow more desirable than she had on the hillside. Gone was the young frightened girl and instead, walking past him, was a confident woman. Her blond hair appeared freshly washed and accented perfectly against the blue silk of her shirt. She once again wore heeled boots to add to her height and they clung to her legs in the same fashion as her flesh-hugging gray denim.

Once in the pub he waited for over an hour before he ventured to her table and now he was being asked point-blank about his intentions. Intentions he still didn't even know or understand.

"I'm getting to know a person who has captured my attention and I hope you're doing the same."

He watched as her flush spread from the valley between her breasts that her shirt exposed upward toward her face. She reached this time for her iced water and he watched her bide her time before answering.

"You have definitely captured my attention. But I'm not sure about why we're bothering to get to know each other."

"You really know how to flatter a man." If he'd thought she'd turned red earlier, she had darkened two shades with his last comment.

"What I meant was that neither of us lives here. We may never even see each other again after tonight."

"Do you want to see me again?"

Another long pause before he heard the small sigh escape her lips before she answered. "I've learned the hard way it doesn't matter what I want."

"It matters to me." And it did. He hated seeing the look of defeat in her eyes and felt as if he would do anything to make it go away.

"And if I did want to see you again?"

"Then we would want the same thing."

He waited for her response, or more so her verbal response. He didn't miss the way her pupils dilated or the slight tremble in her response to him. "I want to see you again. I just don't know if it is a good idea."

"Why wouldn't it be?"

"Because things I thought were right for me in the past have been anything but."

"You don't think you can trust me?"

She wasn't ready for this. She wasn't ready for Ryan. Why now? Except she couldn't really begrudge his arrival in her life, because without him there was the possibility she wouldn't be alive. Could she trust him? Her instincts said yes, but she had been so wrong before that the person she really couldn't trust was herself.

"I don't know what to think about any of this."

"What does your gut tell you?"

Her gut told her that she wanted more. More of Ryan and more of the feelings he was bringing out in her. That even talking to him felt so different from her beginnings with Kevin. She didn't feel that sense of being charmed and swept off her feet, which ironically felt better. Ryan made her feel as if this was less about him and more about her and him liking what he saw in her. What would be the harm in spending more time together? To indulge in the feelings he brought out in her? Her first fling and in less than a week they would go their separate ways, and at best he would become a beautiful memory to carry with her as she carved out her new life. At worst, well, really, what couldn't she face after everything she had already been through?

"It's getting late and it's pretty dark out. Would you mind walking me back to the hotel?"

"I think I can do that."

He signaled to the waitress and paid their bill, silencing her objections to his generosity. She also wasn't able to slip past his gallantry as he helped her put on her jacket and held the door for her as they ventured into the slightly cooled night air.

"It is beautiful here, both day and night," she remarked, feeling relaxation take hold of her for the first time since arriving earlier that day. A yawn escaped her as the jet lag she had been waiting for did the same.

"Careful, these roads are charming but a bit uneven." His words were followed by his arm brushing past hers to take hold of her hand. It was the second time she had felt held to him and she allowed herself to enjoy it.

They walked the few blocks toward the hotel and her mind began to quiet as she enjoyed the evening and her time with Ryan. "It's nice to have someone to look out for me," she thought and said simultaneously.

The hand that had so strongly held hers pulled her toward him as they stopped still in the darkness a few meters from the hotel's entrance. "I wish I could say that all I want to do is look out for you." His voice, sounding slightly anguished, made the short voyage to her ears.

"What do you want to do with me?" she asked, surprised, with no essence of the "come-hither" that question would normally hold.

"This," he answered, as his hands moved even closer to hold her against him as his lips descended on hers. His lips were hard yet so soft against her own and she welcomed the contact. She reached up, letting her hands rest against his chest, loving the feel of his firm chest as much as she enjoyed the pressure of his kiss. She felt his desire for more and she wanted the same, opening her mouth to his for him to explore. She wasn't sure how long they stood like that, in the night, kissing, but she was certain that she had never been kissed like that before.

When they finally broke apart she felt breathless

and dizzy, both in a very good way. "Thank you," she murmured against him.

"Thank you?" he said, puzzled.

"I needed to be kissed like that."

"I'd be happy to do it again."

She laughed and she enjoyed the sound echoing through the night.

"Really, Erin. I have full intentions of kissing you again," he stated outright, and she had no doubt of his plans.

"Can you meet me tomorrow?" she asked with a little hesitancy, hoping for the response she realized she desperately wanted.

"Yes."

"Then I have no doubt you will make good on your promise. Good night. I'll see you in the morning." This time she initiated the kiss as she closed the gap between them once again and softly pressed her lips to his, before breaking away and moving through the hotel courtyard to the entrance. He didn't follow her, which was good as she wasn't sure she would be able to resist any further advances.

Ryan walked onto the balcony of his suite, which in the daytime gave him both a clear view of old Edinburgh and the sea. He sipped from a short glass of Scotch and tried to organize his thoughts and motivations.

He could no longer pretend that he was spending time with Erin to protect her from herself. Did she have a hint of sadness to her—yes. But after tonight he couldn't make the argument that she was depressed and needed saving from herself. Maybe he had misinterpreted what had happened on Arthur's Seat. What he hadn't misinterpreted was his attraction to her. Tonight in the restaurant with every word that had come from her perfectly formed lips and every small move of her body toward him he'd felt a pull toward her. He had meant what he'd said to her—she was beautiful and she said what she meant, and he valued both qualities equally. So much so that he had kissed her and now wanted more.

He looked out into the night and had to blink before he believed what his eyes were showing him. On the balcony a few rooms away he saw Erin. She had changed into a dark-colored nightshirt that seemed to come just to the tops of her bare legs. It was loose on her but between the V-shaped cut of the neckline, its short length and the way a mild wind was pressing it against her he thought it was the sexiest bedtime apparel he had ever seen on a woman. He watched her, half mesmerized by her appearance and half concerned about her choice of location. What was she doing on the balcony? He exhaled a sigh of relief as she reached for a large blanket and wrapped her body in it before taking a seat in one of the balcony chairs, where she stayed staring out into the night.

Ryan, Erin thought, was she ready for Ryan? She had only said goodbye to him a few minutes ago and she already missed him, a man she just met. It was hard to reconcile all the feelings she was experiencing. One of the emotions she had felt during her divorce had been fear. Fear that outside her relationship with Kevin she had no experience with other men. Would another man find her attractive one day? And would she ever trust another man enough? And even if he did and she did, would she ever want the man she loved to suffer the same cruel fate she had been dealt? No.

But Ryan. Did she trust Ryan—yes. But were they ever going to be in a relationship—no. This was a brief and fleeting opportunity and one she didn't feel she could turn away. Because she liked Ryan and the way he made her feel and because she was not going to let Kevin take one more thing from her.

Kevin had been a mistake from the beginning. She had just been too young and naive to see it. She had been a medical student on her first clinical rotation in Orthopedics when she'd met him. She had been nervous and excited, wearing her white clinical jacket for the first time and being called student intern. Everyone had seemed more important than her—the nurses, the residents, the staff physicians—and all she had wanted to do was to impress.

Then she'd met Kevin, or Dr. Dufour, her supervising resident, and he had seemed godlike in comparison to her lowly medical student ranking. He would single her out from her colleagues, giving her more opportunities and one-on-one time than any of the other students on the rotation. At first she had been flattered and had done her best to impress him, going that extra mile to stay late and check bloodwork or making food runs to bring to him in the operating room in between cases. Looking back on it, she had been more his slave than his student, but she had been so in awe of everything he'd represented.

Then his attention had become more personal than professional. Subtle touches, comments on her appearance, and she'd continued to be flattered. She had never been involved with anyone older than her and the attention of an older accomplished man had been absorbing. And he'd been a charmer, a snake charmer, really. It hadn't been long before she'd fallen for him and he'd been making late-night appearances at her apartment. She had been in love with the man she'd thought he was and he had been willing to take advantage.

Until—until she'd become pregnant. And until he'd realized that while her last name was the same as her birth father's, Madden, her stepfather was Dr. Williamson, the hospital's chief of staff. That had been when she'd started getting glimpses of the man he really was, but she had been so overwhelmed with concern over her own life and how the pregnancy was going to affect her career that she'd pushed them to the back of her mind.

The same was done with her hesitancy over getting married. Her parents had made it clear that she had already disappointed them and it had been crushing knowledge, so she'd gone along with their demands, thinking that once Kevin got used to the idea of their upcoming family he would settle into their life together.

She had been so wrong. Once they'd married he'd become resentful and disinterested and she'd become trapped and alone. He hadn't even been there when she'd almost died from complications from her miscarriage. To him it had been the final nail in the coffin that was his marriage. He'd felt unable to leave her now, not if he wanted his career. So he'd stayed. She had tried to make him happy. Tried to regain what they had lost, spending months—years—trying to conceive again, but she couldn't.

Then had come the women. She'd met his first girl-friend shortly after they'd married, learning that he had been involved with the other woman at the same time as her up until their wedding. When she'd confronted him he'd told her what she'd wanted to hear and had promised his fidelity. Soon she had been too caught up in her own pain from her pregnancy loss to care whether he was telling the truth.

But as she had risen from her grief and begun to face her reality, she couldn't hide the signs. By then she had graduated medical school and was now the resident at Boston General and Kevin was a staff orthopedic surgeon. When she walked the halls she would notice people taking more notice of her than was normal. When she entered the emergency department she would see nurses turn and speak quietly to one another. Then finally after three years of marriage she received a written note in her locker from "a friend" who wanted her to know that her husband was sleeping with one of the hospital pharmacists.

He didn't even deny it. Instead he blamed his infidelity on her inadequacies as a wife. In some ways Kevin still won in their divorce. She filed for divorce citing irreconcilable differences, too embarrassed to have her husband's cheating and her deficiencies aired publically. His professional reputation remained intact and he was able to carry on at Boston General as if nothing had happened. Meanwhile, she was struggling to gain her own reputation outside her infamous failed marriage and position as the chief of staff's stepdaughter.

Kevin wanted her gone, completely, and communicated more with her postdivorce with his badgering than he had in the year prior to their ultimate divorce. And it would be easier for her just to leave and start over somewhere new with all her baggage left behind, but there was something about Boston General that felt like home and she wasn't ready to give up anything else in her life.

The wind picked up again and she felt the corners of the blanket lift. It was time to try to sleep, to force herself onto Scottish time. She rose from her chair and peered into the night, instinctively turning to her right, looking away from the ocean and at one of the neighboring balconies. She recognized Ryan. The backlighting of his suite and the darkness of the balcony created the same effect as when she had first seen him and the image of masculine perfection was unchanged. They were too far apart for words, so instead she pressed her hand to her lips and extended it toward him before walking back into her suite and closing the balcony door.

CHAPTER THREE

NERVOUS ANTICIPATION FILLED her as Erin dressed for the unknown in the day ahead. Somehow in the heat of her moment with Ryan they had not made true plans for today, she had just asked him to meet her. When? Where? She had no idea, but she had complete faith that she would see him.

She ran her fingers through her hair, deciding to leave it down, and took a look at her appearance in the mirror. It had felt great that morning, getting ready and knowing that there was someone waiting for her who would be appreciative of her effort. Her cream tunic top had a crocheted design that while it covered her it also revealed her shape beneath. The same went for her gray slim-fit summer pants that ended a few inches above her ankles. She had small slip-on shoes that matched and would be perfect for exploring Edinburgh. She hoped she would see Ryan sooner rather than later.

He was waiting in the hotel lobby when the elevator doors opened. He looked up and smiled, sipping from a takeaway cup of coffee. He looked as good as when she had twice previously seen him. He was freshly washed and shaved and the V-neck of his red polo shirt revealed the hint of another tattoo on his chest. She walked toward him and he rose to greet her, and before she could wish him good morning his lips were against hers. The kiss was brief but no less exciting. "I've been waiting to do that."

"I hope I haven't kept you waiting too long."

"You're worth waiting for. I brought you a coffee. I hope you drink coffee."

"I live on it, thanks."

"So what is your plan for the day?" he asked.

"My plan?" Her only plan had been to be with Ryan.

"Well, my plan was to be with you, which I have now accomplished, so now we move on to your plan."

She knew she was smiling like a fool, but still couldn't change the way she felt. "Ah. Okay, then. Today is my only free day and my plan was to explore Edinburgh. I would be very pleased if you joined me."

"Lead on."

With a genuine smile she led them back outside the hotel, where Ryan took her hand. "Let me guess, we're going to the princess castle."

"Of course," she replied, and felt by the time the day was done her whole face was going to hurt from the happiness Ryan seemed to be able to bring out in her. "But don't worry, the princess castle also contains the military museum, which should appease you."

They made their way through the irregular streets toward the Edinburgh Castle entrance. She knew not to object as Ryan paid their entrance fee and they passed through the castle gate. "Look up," he instructed.

Above them was a spiked portcullis designed to

protect the castle against siege. "Not exactly a fairy-tale castle feature," he added.

"I don't believe in fairy tales."

"Another thing we have in common, because neither do I."

Ryan held her hand as they passed in and out of the buildings that made up Edinburgh Castle. She had always enjoyed history and was happy that Ryan also seemed fascinated by the depth of history within the castle walls. They took their time exploring the National War Museum and she was impressed with his knowledge as he took the time to explain to her the nuances of past wars. At the end of the museum was a new exhibit dedicated to war veterans with amputations and the use of prosthetics.

"Amazing, isn't it?" Ryan remarked, as they examined the cabinet filled with examples of modern bionic limbs.

"It is."

"I should have been an orthopedic surgeon," he remarked, not knowing the effect his words would have on her.

"No, you shouldn't have been," she blurted, not able to censor herself yet again.

"Why not?" he asked, confused by the shift in her demeanor.

"Because I like you just the way you are," she answered, trying to cover the real meaning behind her remark.

"Why do I feel like there is something you are not saying?"

She sighed, realizing that her deflection hadn't

worked and she was going to have to bring her past into what was already the best day she'd had in years.

"Because there is. My ex-husband is an orthopedic surgeon and I would like to think that you have nothing in common."

"Ah. So you have a thing against doctors?" She could tell he was testing her and she hoped she didn't sound like a bitter, scorned woman.

"That would make my life very hard, considering I am one. I've just learned the hard way about the dangers of mixing personal and professional lives and would never risk that again." She watched him, waiting for his reaction, and didn't miss the conflict in his face. Was he so surprised that she was a physician or was he just as bothered as she was that her ex had entered into their time together. She wanted to go back and take away her comment. "Besides, the only type of man I could now ever imagine being attracted to is one in the military."

She smiled, and her smile only grew as he smiled back at her.

"Is that so?"

"Absolutely and completely."

"So doctors are not your type?"

"Nope, I only have eyes for ruggedly handsome soldiers who save my life and come with no strings attached." As the words left her lips even she didn't doubt her sincerity. Ryan was the complete opposite of Kevin and the possibility of something between them felt more and more right with every moment they spent together. He was what she needed, a couple of days of abandon to restore everything her failed marriage had taken away from her.

The way he looked at her she had no doubt he was feeling the same attraction she was. "Well, Dr. Erin, I think we are both fortunate that you have equally opened my eyes to the appeal of female physicians. So I take it you are not in orthopedics. What do you do?"

"Obstetrics and gynecology."

"That would be the opposite of orthopedics," he remarked, and she appreciated that he, too, was trying to lighten the mood.

"It's less complicated than taking care of men." She laughed.

"Ouch." He feigned injury.

"It is actually amazing helping women and being there for one of the most special times in their lives."

"Did you know that Mary Queen of Scots gave birth in this castle?"

"No, I didn't."

"Then let's go check out the birth chamber of James VI." He once again connected his hand with hers and she marveled at how the same action brought even more excitement each time he touched her.

She had been right. Her face hurt from smiling. As they toured the entire castle she felt completely at peace and in her element, learning about Scottish history and with a man she respected and whose company she enjoyed. Not to mention an attraction that was growing exponentially. Every time he reached for her hand it felt as if they were connecting and throughout the day she was holding her breath, waiting for the moment when he would kiss her again.

She felt the first drop hit her shoulder as they once again passed through the castle gates. Then the second, then the third. Within seconds the sky had opened and rain was pouring down on both of them. She felt a tug on her hand as he pulled her into the protection of a narrow corridor between the old brick buildings. The small space necessitated being pressed together and any thoughts she had of being cold immediately vanished. Ryan's hand swept her wet bangs from her forehead before his lips came down on hers.

Finally, she thought as she met him with equal passion. His lips were wet with the rain and added to the freshness of his taste. She opened her mouth to him, wanting more, and was rewarded by his response. His tongue met hers until she didn't know where he ended and she began. At the same time his hands trailed from his initial position on her face along the sides of her body until she felt them on her bare back underneath the dampness of her shirt. Another point of heat between them.

She wanted more. Wanted him to move his hands over her and caress her aching breasts. Wanted to feel the ultimate fulfillment that the rigidity pressed into her abdomen promised.

"Not here," he murmured into her ear, when they finally broke apart.

She looked into the pouring rain. "Want to make a run for it?"

"Yes," he agreed with the same smile she had become accustomed to.

She kissed him once more, pressing her lips to his with the firm passion that had ignited inside her, before they broke apart and made their start on the sprint back to the hotel. It took them ten minutes but on arrival in the hotel's lobby she was completely soaked through and panting from the exertion of their run.

She followed Ryan's lead and they said nothing to each other, the understanding already present between them as they entered the elevator and Ryan pressed the button for his floor. As soon as the door closed they were once again wrapped around each other. His lips were on hers. His hands were covering her body. And she was burning up despite the cold, wet clothing covering them both.

As the doors opened they broke apart and with one mutual look their sprint continued hand in hand. One swipe of Ryan's key and they were tumbling into his room. They reunited in their embrace, but this time there were no restrictions from being in a public place to hold them back. She watched as he pulled away from their kiss and peeled his soaked shirt from his body. It felt like an unveiling as she got to see first-hand what lay beneath.

Nothing disappointed. Every muscle on his body was defined. The tattoo she had seen hints of on his chest was a serpent entwined on a single rod along his right pectoral muscle. It reminded her of the caduceus, the symbol she recognized for medicine, but it was slightly different. Encircling his right biceps was another design. Either way she had never considered tattoos attractive but on Ryan they were explosive.

Before she could enjoy him any further she felt herself being stripped of her drenched top. She had previously been shy about her body, but not with Ryan. The minute she was exposed she wasn't because he pressed back against her. His mouth rejoined hers but it wasn't long before he was trailing his lips down her neck to her shoulder. She threaded her fingers through his wet hair and felt her body melting into his.

His hands skimmed her back before she felt the clasp of her bra release and the weight of her breasts released from their confines. Yes, she thought, this was what she wanted. He stepped back from her and she was rewarded by the look in his eye and the knowledge that he was every bit as enthralled as she was. With painstaking precision he eased the garment from her shoulders, down her arms and completely off, before he skimmed her breasts with the back of his hand. It was seduction at its finest. Then without pause he was against her, lifting her, his hands cupping her bottom before resting her on the dresser's edge. The move had made up for their foot difference in height and she felt even closer to him.

She was finally rewarded with the feel of both of his hands, each cupping a breast and causing electric shocks of want to course through her body to her core. His hands gently caressed her as his mouth returned to her neck, his thumbs occasionally brushing against the peaks of her rigid nipples. She loved every touch, welcomed it as she felt the anticipation of what was still to come.

He paused his tactile exploration and she opened her eyes to see why he'd stopped. His hand was able to completely cover her own tattoo, a small willow tree on her lower left hip. She blinked hard, thinking about what it represented, not wanting to explain its significance, especially now.

"You're beautiful."

And she believed him. "Thank you."

* * *

A weeping willow, he thought to himself, and instantly the memory of her vulnerability on the hillside played in his mind. What was he doing? He thought to himself. He wanted her, desperately, but was this fair to her? When he knew she was vulnerable? No, it wasn't fair to her, and from what he had learned about her so far she both needed, and deserved, someone to be on her side.

"I think we should slow down." The words were torn from him because it was what his rational thought wanted but not what his body wanted.

"What?" she said. Her eyes dilated in both passion and disbelief.

He couldn't repeat himself so instead he reached into one of the nearby dressers and pulled out a T-shirt, which he proceeded to cover her with. He needed to cover the temptation she represented—it didn't work. She still turned him on and now she looked hurt and that was the last thing he wanted.

"I don't want us to do anything you are going to regret."

"Why would I regret this?"

He wanted to be as honest as she had been. Because he was a physician and she didn't know. Because maybe her deeply hidden sadness was making her vulnerable to him. "Because I'm worried I'm taking advantage of you."

He watched as her arms crossed protectively across her chest and she ran a hand through her hair, which had become wild as it dried from the rain. "In what way?"

"In that I saved your life and maybe you feel indebted to me."

"I don't. I'm grateful, but I don't."

"Okay, but what about the fact that you admitted you were running away from a disaster in your life?"

"I think that's for me to worry about."

"Not just you, Erin."

"I think I should go."

He instinctively lifted her down from the dresser he had perched her on and backed away. He watched as she looked at the wet heap that was her shirt and bra on the floor before deciding to leave it and making her way to the door.

She shut the door of her room and collapsed against the back of it before sinking down on the floor. He hadn't stopped her and he hadn't followed her, and how she had wanted him to. The worst part was that she believed him and understood why he had stopped.

Ryan saw her as fragile and he didn't want to take advantage of her. Where had he been three years ago? And how she wished he had been wrong, but the truth was she was still vulnerable. And maybe she would always have that vulnerability that had been born from being broken.

Was she making a good decision with Ryan? She knew she wanted him and wished he hadn't stopped what had been the most sensual encounter she had ever experienced. But she also couldn't deny that she wasn't in a good position emotionally to be making major life choices. But was Ryan that? She had convinced herself last night that he was a holiday indulgence to be enjoyed but after today he felt like more. And what was worse, she actually respected and trusted him more for turning her away. So where did that leave them now?

CHAPTER FOUR

A KNOCK AT HER hotel room door roused her from the late-afternoon nap she had been indulging in. After she had lifted herself from the room's floor and showered the chill from her body she curled up in the hotel-provided terry-toweling robe, thinking of all the questions she had no answers for.

She fastened the robe's sash tightly and then made her way to the door. She opened the door slightly to see Ryan, who also looked drier than the last time she had seen him. She opened the door wider and stepped aside to allow him inside. Both her eyes and her nose spotted the bag of food he was carrying.

"I thought I would bring dinner to you."

She glanced at the room's clock and realized that her late-afternoon nap had spread well into the evening and it was past eight.

"Thank you," she said cautiously, not knowing where they stood. "How did you know which room I was in?"

"I saw you last night on your balcony and you're welcome." He went ahead and set up his offering on the round table adjacent to the glass balcony doors and she took the seat intended for her.

"Smells delicious," she remarked, trying to keep their conversation neutral but realizing she was more than happy at his reappearance.

"It's nice to see you smile. I was worried I had ruined things between us."

His confession brought out an instant relaxation in her and the awkwardness of the aftermath of the previous encounter dissolved.

"You haven't."

"I hope you like traditional Scottish fare. It was what the restaurant recommended and it seemed fitting. Plus they had the bread pudding that you seemed very fond of last night." He was smiling to accompany the gentle familiarity of his teasing.

"You know what they say about holidays—it's the time to indulge."

"Yes." His voice had changed and contained a masculine huskiness as she realized the other meanings of her words. It was clear that, whatever had happened between them, he still wanted her, too.

"So what are your plans?" she asked, trying to shift the focus from their almost sexual encounter.

He choked on the glass of water he had been sipping from. "Excuse me?"

"For the rest of your time in Scotland," she amended, realizing he'd thought she had been asking about his plans for her.

"I have a commitment the day after tomorrow and then I have to return to the base. What are your plans, Erin?"

"Today was my last free day."

"I refuse to accept that."

"I'm afraid it's true. I have two days of meetings then I'm flying back to the States the next morning."

"But your nights are free?"

"That depends. Why did you stop earlier?" She needed to know. She wasn't prepared to spend more time torturing herself by being with Ryan and wondering how he felt about her and what his intentions were.

"I thought we had covered that."

"What if I wanted to readdress it?"

"Your tattoo."

"What?" She didn't understand his comment.

"Your tattoo."

"Considering your own ink, I'm surprised you have a problem with a woman having a tattoo."

"I don't. I actually think it's beautiful. You can tell that you had it placed for only you to see."

"I did." How did this man read her so well?

"It's a weeping willow, and it reminded me that the one thing I don't want to do is hurt you."

"So don't." She was rewarded with his smile. "Did you know weeping willows are known for their tenacious roots that continue life, but the trees themselves are also a symbol of compassion? My tattoo symbolizes tenacity and compassion, both qualities of the weeping willow and both qualities I strive to possess."

"You don't think you already do?"

"I think, to be the person I want to be and the physician I want to be, I need to work on both."

"I like you the way you are."

It was what she needed to hear after years of being not enough for a husband who hadn't valued or loved her. Ryan's words empowered her. "Thank you. I feel the same way about you. What if I told you you were what I needed? Would that change your mind?"

"Explain." She saw him shifting in his chair and knew she had gotten through to him.

"Maybe what I need is time with a man I respect and who actually renews my faith in men and maybe myself."

"I'm a soldier, first and foremost. I couldn't promise you anything."

"I don't want you to promise me anything. I've been promised the world by a man and it didn't work out. So you don't need to worry about not giving me a promise for forever because even if you did I wouldn't accept it."

"Are you sure?"

"Yes."

He stood from his chair opposite her and she took a deep breath of anticipation until he started walking away from her. "If you are still sure tomorrow then I'll pick you up at seven tomorrow night. If you change your mind, please just stand me up so that I don't try to change it back."

She watched mutely as he walked away and then was surprised when he suddenly turned back. She felt him lift her from her chair and gather her in his arms before his lips made contact with hers. It was hot, it was hard and it was every bit as passionate as she wanted. When he broke away she was gasping for air but still not wanting it to have ended.

"Just in case you needed a reminder. Good night, sleep tight."

How was she ever going to make it until seven tonight? A restless night, thinking of the possibilities, had left her completely devoid of sleep. Added to that, she seemed to have forgotten the skill of being able to sit through hours of seminars and she had no ability to focus on the lectures being presented. The International Society of Obstetrics and Gynecology conference had been her original reason for the trip to Scotland but now it was the furthest thing from her mind.

She had been elected to sit on a discussion panel throughout the conference to provide a perspective on both the American experience and the experience of the younger generation of obstetricians and gynecologists. At the time it had been an honor, but now all she could think of was Ryan.

"Dr. Dufour." A voice cut into her thoughts and she instantly recoiled inwardly. She had registered for the conference before her name had legally returned to her maiden name of Madden.

"Yes," she answered reluctantly.

"What has been your experience in the States with single embryo transfers to reduce the rates of multiple births in infertile couples?"

She did her best to shift her focus away from the nervous anticipation of the upcoming night and back to her original purpose for being in Scotland. She needed to focus on her work, particularly as infertility was her area of interest and she was looking for a fellowship in that area after graduation.

She straightened her navy blazer and took a sip of water before turning on the power to the microphone in front of her. "The single embryo transfer program is a much better option for women whose treatment cycles are funded through government insurance programs. In the United States women still pay out of their own pockets for their cycles, most of the time taking on significant debt for the chance at a baby. Given those circumstances, it is hard to convince them to transfer just one embryo."

"What about the ability to reduce the rate of multiple births?"

She thought back to the aftermath of her miscarriage and the months, years, she'd spent trying for another baby. If she had naturally become pregnant with twins she would have cried with joy. It would have felt as if she was being compensated for the baby she'd lost and the suffering she had endured. Instead nothing, every month nothing, and instead she had felt punished. Punished for unwittingly being the other woman. She should never have been with Kevin. She didn't deserve a baby.

"As obstetricians we have firsthand knowledge of the risks of twins and most of us would not want to roll the dice with the risks of extreme prematurity and the resulting possibility of lifelong complications. Women with infertility feel very differently. They would take any risk for the chance at a child and no amount of counseling from us on the risk of multiple births is going to change that."

She tried her best to actively follow the panel discussion and not fall back into her own thoughts. But she was speaking from personal experience. She knew the risks of twins and still she would have happily rolled the dice for a baby. Babies. It had taken a long time before she had accepted that the life-threatening infection she had experienced after her miscarriage had permanently damaged her so that she would never have a child.

Acceptance of that harsh reality had been one of the reasons she had finally gathered the courage up to leave Kevin. She had realized that one of the reasons she had looked the other way from her suspicions of his infidelity was because she'd seen him as her way to have a baby. When her dreams of being a mother had been lost, she'd no longer had any need to pretend, even to herself, that she was happy in her marriage.

"I'd like to thank the panel for their experience and participation in today's discussion. We will resume tomorrow morning with our special guest speaker and headline symposium 'Postpartum Hemorrhage—Tales from the Battlefield,'" the moderator announced.

Erin snapped back to the present and glanced at her watch. It was four-thirty. That left two and a half hours until Ryan met her. How was she going to make it till then without going crazy?

She left the conference center and made her way to a nearby café. The sun was setting and the streets of Edinburgh appeared enchanting before her, as if they had a promise of something to offer. She ordered a latte, hoping the caffeine would help ground her, before settling into a corner table and dialing.

"Hey, Erin," the voice on the other end of the phone welcomed her warmly, and she instantly felt her nerves settle. It was hard to be infamous and make friends. Most of her fellow residents were intimidated by the fact that she was the chief of staff's stepdaughter. The others were too busy enjoying the gossip her dysfunctional marriage had created to get to know her. But Chloe Darcy was different. She was unthreatened by all Erin's baggage and instead Erin felt as if she had really gained a true friend.

"Hi, Chloe."

"I'd like to think you are calling just to chat and tell me how wonderful Scotland is, but I have a feeling there's something more."

"I met a guy," Erin confessed.

"Um, not what I was expecting to hear, but I'm absolutely thrilled!" Erin could tell she was being genuine. "So who is he?"

"His name is Ryan, he's in the military and he saved my life."

"Are you being literal or figurative?"

"Literal. I was walking on a hillside known as Arthur's Seat when the wind blew me right off. Ryan found me clinging to the hill's edge and pulled me to safety."

"But you are okay now?"

"Yes."

"Wow, that's scary and also incredibly romantic. So, aside from being a hero, what is he like?"

"Honest, kind and interested in me and not himself."

"Sounds perfect."

"It's not forever."

"He sounds perfect. Why don't you just see how things go and not worry about forever?"

"Because not worrying has previously been my downfall."

"I'm not going to disagree with that one. I'm actually not sure you could have picked a more horrible man to marry."

"Has he been hitting on you again?" Erin asked.

Chloe was easily one of the most beautiful women Erin had ever met and was often on the receiving end of unwanted attention. Erin knew that Kevin had made passes at her even before they'd separated.

"Don't worry about it. It's nothing I can't handle. So what is the plan with hero Ryan?"

"He's coming to my hotel room tonight."

"And?"

"And anything beyond that is my decision. He's afraid of taking advantage of me, and quite frankly I'm worried I'm not ready. I might get hurt."

"But you don't want forever and this guy makes you feel happy and valued, right?"

"Yes."

"Are you wanting me to tell you what to do?"

"Yes."

"Well, then, that's easy! Go for it. If you didn't want to you never would have called me. I'm your enabler friend."

Erin smiled and felt herself nodding in agreement, even though Chloe couldn't see her. Maybe her life was coming around. In Chloe she had a friend she needed and now she was on the verge of a romantic liaison with a man who enthralled her.

"Thanks, you're a great friend."

"So are you. Do what feels right and if you want to talk I'm always only a phone call away."

Erin said her goodbyes, hung up the call and finished her latte, then made her way back to her room. Once inside she slipped into the bathroom and drew herself a hot bath, which she soaked in for another hour. Once the water had cooled considerably she forced herself to get out, and proceeded through all her typical rituals, drawing them out as much as she could. She applied lotion to her entire body. She dried her hair in sections, curling the ends under with her round brush. For makeup she decided to keep it neutral and applied only a layer of mascara to her eyelashes and a gloss to her lips. When she looked up in the mirror she liked what she saw.

She moved toward the closet and examined her options. She had packed for a conference, not for this, whatever this was going to be. She selected some of the clothes she had brought for travel. A pair of black footless tights over which she layered two tank tops, black with blue over top. Given her short stature, both ended over her hips. She had a long string of silver beads, which completed the outfit, and Erin was pleased when she saw her reflection. She glanced at her watch. Six fifty-eight.

Two minutes passed slowly, but it was only two minutes, because exactly at seven a knock sounded on the door. She took a deep breath before slowly making her way to the door. Ryan stood there, his white dress shirt layered with a black cable sweater. There were leather patches on the elbows and he had an overall look of sophistication, which she appreciated.

"Hi," she opened hesitantly.

He walked toward her, placing his hands on her arms and his lips on hers. He tasted of mint and felt like heaven. The kiss was romantic and passionate, true bliss. If this was how they would spend their night together, even this would be enough.

"I'm glad you're here."

"It's my room. Where else would I be?"

"You could have gotten cold feet."

"That was you, not me." She watched as he understood her meaning.

"Yes, but you need to know it won't happen again." He was giving her one last warning. One last chance to back out.

"Glad to hear it," she whispered, as this time she leaned toward him and pressed her lips against his. What she meant as sweet acceptance quickly changed. He matched the pressure she had exerted and her mouth opened to his instinctively. He tasted her and she reveled in his exploration. She ran her hand down his slightly raspy cheek and his hands slipped around her, pinning her to him and settling on her lower back. She was shocked when she heard herself purring against him and felt the smile that came to his lips.

"This wasn't my plan," he murmured against her.

"It wasn't?" She couldn't keep the disappointment from her voice.

"Well, it was, but later in the evening after I'd had the opportunity to wine and dine you."

"Then wine and dine away, as long as you and I are both clear on how this is all going to end tonight." She wasn't sure who was more surprised at her words, him or her. Gone was the shy, inexperienced girl she had been a few years ago. Ryan made her feel like a mature, confident woman and it was a feeling she found herself very much enjoying.

"Wow" was all Ryan could think. The small part of him that was still warning him that Erin was more vulnerable than she was letting on was being slowly eroded by the confident, sexual woman before him.

When had been the last time he had been this en-thralled by a woman? The answer was never. Every-thing about her—her honesty, her beauty, her open sexuality—was causing havoc with his cautious con-science.

"You are doing your best to ruin my good inten-tions." In more ways than one, he thought to himself.

"Good," she purred.

He had to force himself to take his hand from her back and instead grab her hand as he quickly guided her out of her hotel room and away from temptation.

They fell into a comfortable silence as they strolled through the night's dusky streets toward the restau-rant he had chosen. Once inside the warmth of the dining room he dismissed the restaurant's host for the pleasure of slipping Erin's light trench coat from her shoulders and pulling out her chair himself.

They both read through the menus but, to be hon-est, he could have ordered dirt and not noticed to-night. "You pick."

"Me?" she asked, looking at him, puzzled.

"You. I want to get to know your tastes."

"I would have thought they were obvious by now. I like men in the military with tattoos and sexy scars on their foreheads."

He instinctively touched the thin silver line that ran on his forehead. "You noticed my scar?"

"It's part of the appeal." She beamed back at him. "How did you get it?"

It was a question he had been asked multiple times and he knew what response she was anticipating. Like everyone else, she probably assumed it was a combat-related injury.

"I was involved in an altercation," he started.

Erin leaned toward him and he could tell she was waiting for the excitement of a battle story. He could see her almost holding her breath as the gentle rise and fall of her breasts ceased.

"With my little sister when I was seven."

Her face froze and then broke into a larger smile as she burst out laughing. She didn't seem at all disappointed by the truth.

"What happened?" she asked.

"I was teasing her and she had enough."

"And…"

"And she threw a solid plastic castle at me. I needed twelve stitches."

He was rewarded again with Erin's laugh, which sounded like soft musical notes. "The worst part was she took it harder than I did and cried for hours."

"Are you close with your sister?"

"Yes, one of the hardest parts of being in the military is the time away from my family. Do you have any brothers or sisters?"

"No. I'm an only child."

"Do you like it?"

He saw the slight change in her as her shoulder fell and her head tilted downward. She took a sip from the water glass in front of her before she answered. "No, it's hard to have all your parents' expectations fall on you."

"But you're a successful physician." And so much more, Ryan thought to himself. How could anyone not be proud of Erin?

"I'm a divorced obstetrician-gynecologist." She

said it as if it made perfect sense but nothing about her words seemed condemning.

"So?"

"My parents are Catholic and don't believe in divorce."

"And?" He could tell there was more she didn't want to say.

"And my stepfather is an orthopedic surgeon and the chief of staff at the hospital where I'm completing my residency."

"In the same department as your ex-husband."

"Yes. And as you pointed out yesterday, orthopedics and obstetrics are about as polar opposite as you can get. I think I disappointed them both with my choice in husband and in my choice of career."

There it was again, that vulnerability. A need for approval. Part of him was pulling back, wanting to be cautious, but the majority of him wanted to help make her see everything he saw in her. "But you have no regrets?"

"About my marriage? Yes. About my career? Never."

"Well, in the end, it sounds to me like you made two very good decisions, since both of them have brought us together."

CHAPTER FIVE

SHE'D NEVER THOUGHT she would ever smile when it came to talking about her marriage, but Ryan had the ability to make her feel differently about her past. His praise was much needed and valued. It didn't feel like pointless flattery. It was obvious respect from a man she felt the same way about.

The waiter came to their table and looked at Ryan expectantly. He gestured toward Erin and she ordered for them both.

"Perfect," Ryan commented, and she felt even more relaxed in his presence.

She spent the rest of the meal conflicted between never wanting it to end and wanting it to end so they could be alone together. Her sense of nervous anticipation only returned as Ryan signed the check and she once again felt her jacket being slipped over her shoulders.

They left the restaurant and she started walking but Ryan, whose hand she was holding, didn't move. She stopped and turned back to look at him, not missing the serious look on his face. "I'm leaving the day after tomorrow."

"I know," she admitted. She found herself not

looking forward to the end of their brief romance but wasn't going to dwell on it.

"I just needed to remind you."

"I know." She knew the type of man Ryan was. Everything he was he put out for the world to see. She closed the distance between them and kissed him, reveling in his response. She didn't know how long they stayed that way, kissing in the moonlight. It was wonderful and only the desire for a different kind of more had her break away.

He seemed to read her mind. "Let's go."

She wasn't sure she even exhaled during the short walk back to the hotel. As they rode up the elevator and hurried down the hall where both their rooms were located, she glanced fleetingly at her hotel room door as they passed it without slowing. Finally the door to Ryan's room was closing and she felt herself let go of the breath she had been holding.

Within seconds she was gasping for air for a different reason as she found herself pressed against the wall, every inch of her body covered with Ryan's. She opened her mouth to his, once again entangling her fingers in his hair as his mouth sealed with hers. As his lips finally left hers and started kissing down the column of her neck he whispered against her skin, "Last chance, Erin."

She reached down under the hem of his sweater, pulling it away from him to allow her hands access to the dress shirt below. She spread her fingers to feel his tight muscles and the radiating heat of his body beneath her hands. "I'm staying."

"Thank God, because there is nothing I want more right now than you."

His comment made her feel bold and she wrenched the sweater over his head and moved her hands to the small shirt buttons. Slowly she started working them open. The most arousing part was Ryan watching her, his pupils dilated, tracking her every movement. The instant she was done he returned the favor, stripping her of her layered tank tops.

His hands tangled in her hair, lifting it and exposing her bare neck. His mouth returned to her neck and she pressed so hard into his body she didn't know where he began and she ended. She felt the tips of his fingers brush upward just below her breasts. Her breasts ached in desperation for his touch. The clasp of her bra opened and she felt just the slightest release of her breasts before Ryan's hands replaced what the white lace had been poorly concealing.

His cupped hands allowed his thumbs to slowly graze her nipples. His lips brushed against her collarbone before she felt her breast being lifted, his lips gentle against the raised mound.

"Perfect." She felt his word vibrate against her sensitized skin. Before she could respond she felt herself being lifted, with Ryan's hands strong against the backs of her thighs as he carried her across the room. The hard wall that had been pressed against her back was replaced with the softness of the linen-covered king-size bed. But she didn't lack for firmness for long as Ryan drew over her.

His attention returned to her as he once again kissed her softly parted lips, drawing her into him.

As much as she hungered for the intense escalation of their passion, she also felt her entire body liquefy with the slow pace that Ryan was setting. His mouth was close to her breasts and as soon as she thought she might die if he didn't, his mouth closed over one nipple as his fingers rolled its companion.

She arched her back in pleasure and she could feel Ryan's upturned smile against her skin. Her nipple felt cold as his mouth left her but her other one was then treated to the same pleasure as he switched sides to give both breasts equal consideration. When she felt as if she could bear no more she reached for his hand and placed it where she wanted him most. She could feel the heat and moisture at the heart of her and hoped he got the message she was desperately, and not so subtly, trying to send.

He did. He pulled away and his hands gathered in her tights, peeling them away until she lay bare before him, aside from the small white lace bikini briefs that matched the previously discarded bra. She pushed herself up on her elbows to watch him undress, the act accomplished in mere seconds as he shed every article of remaining clothing until he stood naked before her.

"Wow." The word left her mouth before she could filter her feelings. It sounded naive even to her ears but she'd had no idea a man could look like that.

"That's what I was thinking about you."

Instantly her embarrassment at her momentary gaucheness fled and her connection to Ryan intensified. He kneeled on the bed before her and without breaking eye contact pulled at the lace of her panties until she was as bare as he was. He braced himself on one arm as his hand laced through her hair and began its gentle caress down her body. His hand was rough against the softness of her neck, the side of her breast, her abdomen, her hip, as it moved inward toward her thigh. She parted her legs, waiting and wanting. With the softest touch she felt him, his fingers first gently parting her and then a gentle stroke.

"Oh," she gasped, not ready for the wave of electricity that passed through her. He responded by reclaiming her mouth and kissing her deeply. Then she felt it again, the wave of pleasure that came as he stroked her, this time in an unending circle. She felt herself wriggling against him but not wanting to get away. A strange tingling intensity was building inside her and she wasn't sure she could bear it. She cried into his mouth until finally every nerve ending from her core exploded outward and she felt beautifully broken. Finally she realized what she had been missing.

"You're beautiful."

"Thank you, but we're so not done here."

"No, we are just getting started."

She watched as he reached into the nightstand and retrieved a small foil packet. "May I?" she asked.

His eyebrows rose, but he agreed by passing her the condom. She carefully opened the packet but before she sheathed him she took hold of him in her hand, wanting to feel what she was visually devouring. He felt hot and hard against her and she squeezed lightly and he hardened further in her hand. "You need to hurry."

She looked at him and felt every bit the temptress. She gently rolled the condom along his length, looking forward to the moment when she could feel him more intimately. As soon as she reached his base she felt herself being pushed back against the blankets, Ryan's hand pulling her leg around him before he surged into her.

It felt like a completely new experience, an experience that was all pleasure. It was as if he had the ability to stretch and mold her into the most perfect state of arousal. She wrapped her other leg around him as he began to move back and forth within her, each time pushing her to a further level of bliss. Then that intense feeling came back, every stroke setting off a chain of sparks that was building a fire at her core. An all-encompassing need for more grew ever stronger within her until she thought she would die if he stopped. But he didn't. He pushed her harder and further until she burst into flames, screaming his name, not even aware of the marks she simultaneously scored down his back.

He cried out against her and she knew it was a cry of pleasure and not of pain as he collapsed against her, his breath rapid and hot on her neck. He appeared as shattered as she was and she ran her fingers more gently up and down his back in a soothing rhythm.

"You're more than perfect, you're amazing," he whispered in her ear.

"I…I…" But she couldn't think.

He kissed her fumbling lips and she closed her eyes in happiness.

She felt him pull away from her and was hoping

and waiting for him to return to hold her. What would it feel like to be held in the aftermath of such bliss?

"Erin, we have a problem." Ryan's voice was as grave as his words and her eyes opened wide. He looked stricken, staring back at her.

"The condom broke," he explained, and she exhaled with a sense of relief.

"It's okay," she tried to assure him.

"No, it's not okay. As much as I care for you, this isn't forever."

It wasn't just what he was saying about the temporary nature of their relationship that burst her bliss bubble, it was the private information that she didn't want to think of and now had to share.

"I can't have children."

"What?" It was now his turn to be taken aback. How she didn't want to talk about this, but she also knew she needed to put his mind at rest so their night together could return to where it had been.

"I had a miscarriage during my marriage. Afterward I developed a severe infection that scarred my Fallopian tubes and uterus. I can't have children."

"Are you sure?" It was a natural question. One she had asked herself over and over again until she had accepted her fate.

"Yes. I wanted a baby very badly and have spent the past two years trying to get pregnant. It's never going to happen. I've accepted that. So you don't need to worry about the condom breaking."

"I'm sorry." It was exactly what she didn't want to hear. She didn't want tonight to be about her past or what she would never have in the future. She just wanted it to be about them and their night together.

She moved herself from the bed and started looking for her clothes.

"What are you doing?"

"I'm…" *Running from a painful truth and your pity.*

"You're not leaving me, not now, not when both you and I know what we can be together."

She looked back at him, looking for any traces of pity left on his face, but she saw none. All she saw was want and so she stayed.

Ryan reached out an arm and was met with air. He opened his eyes and searched for her, but it was clear she wasn't there. He had planned on telling her more about himself and why he was in Edinburgh, but the moment had never presented itself.

Between making love and holding her as they'd rested between bouts of rapture he had let the night slip away. When he had awoken that morning she was gone and all that remained was a note.

Ryan, thought you deserved the rest. Please come and find me tonight for a last night together—Erin.

Now he had no choice, he glanced at the clock and knew he wouldn't have time to talk to her privately in person. Still, after their night together he had no doubt that nothing could break the bond and trust they had formed.

Erin couldn't recall when she had last felt this happy. She had slipped from her lover's bed in the early hours of the morning and had hopes of returning to it as soon as she completed her work.

She straightened the black blazer that overlaid a cream lace camisole and her favorite strand of pearls. She had one more symposium before she knew Ryan would find her. She had never felt this free before. A feeling of wild recklessness filled her as she glanced nervously around the room. She hadn't prepared for today's session. Every thought and action had been about Ryan last night and she had forgone any thought of reading through the presentation or even the speaker's background information she had been provided with. She took her seat on the stage, sipping from a glass of the iced water before her to chill the heated thoughts Ryan provoked.

"Ladies and gentlemen, thank you for joining us for our final session, 'Postpartum Hemorrhage—Tales from the Battleground.' Our special guest speaker today is Dr. Ryan Callum. Dr. Callum is a medical officer in the American military. Having served on front lines for the past twelve years, he has developed firsthand experience in the management of massive bleeding and transfusion. This knowledge is becoming more and more relevant to the field of obstetrics, where acuity is forever increasing and particularly our management of postpartum hemorrhage, which, despite our best efforts, we have not been able to decrease the incidence of. Today Dr. Callum is going to shift our attention beyond prevention to optimum management to ensure patient well-being. Everyone, please welcome Dr. Ryan Callum."

All of a sudden the moderator had her absolute attention as she replayed everything he had just said.

His name was Ryan, he was in the military… She watched the entrance, desperately hoping to see someone other than her Ryan. But as the door opened her sense of dread ballooned into extreme hurt as her Ryan walked through the doors. Dr. Ryan Callum was just that, a doctor. Why hadn't he told her? How could he have held something back when she had bared her soul and innermost pain to him?

Had he just told her what she'd wanted to hear, just as Kevin had? He had to have known the conference was why she was in Edinburgh and that she would find out that he was also a physician. Why wouldn't he have told her instead of the public humiliation of learning who your lover really was in front of hundreds of people? It didn't bother her that he was a physician; it bothered her that she felt she had been lied to, even if by omission. The trust that had built between them vanished in an instant and her heart, body and mind felt instantly on guard against this man whom she had briefly let in. She had been a fool, again.

Ryan took his place at the podium and she could feel his eyes on her, but she couldn't turn to look at him.

"Dr. Callum," the moderator continued, "allow me to introduce your panel. Dr. Nicholas Richter. Dr. Richter is the head of Maternal Fetal Medicine at St. Bishop's Hospital in London. Dr. Mary Ellison. Dr. Ellison is a community obstetrician-gynecologist from Canada and also has an extensive background in global obstetrics and gynecology, spearheading multiple international projects around the world. And Dr. Erin Dufour. Dr. Dufour is a resident in obstetrics and gynecology from Boston, Massachusetts. She has been kind enough to provide us with insight both from the American and the younger generation's experience."

At this point she could no longer stare ahead and forced herself to turn her eyes to his. She saw something she had never seen before in his eyes—anger. Confusion and an equal anger set in. What did Ryan have to be angry about? He was the liar. He was the one who had betrayed her trust.

It was the longest ninety minutes of her life. As Ryan talked she had the utmost difficulty focusing on his words. She was aware the panel had started talking and any minute she could be called on to comment.

"Dr. Dufour, do you think there is a need in American centers to adopt the massive transfusion protocol Dr. Callum has discussed today?"

She wanted to refuse to have anything more to do with anything related to Dr. Callum but she managed to swallow her personal feelings and focus on being professional. "As we heard from the outset of today's lecture, we have not been able to reduce the incidence of postpartum hemorrhage in the past ten years. Even when we know the risks are present, all we can do is hope that it doesn't happen to our patients. Having more options for treatment is something every obstetrician would embrace in order to decrease the morbidity we often feel helpless to prevent."

A discussion continued on optimal implementation and the availability of resources in smaller centers. Erin was thinking of her own words. Had she known she could get hurt becoming involved with Ryan? Yes, and no. Yes, it was always a possibility in any relationship, but she had never considered it to be a real possibility, not with Ryan. He had seemed so honest, so genuine in his interest in her best interests. And the things she had told him, everything about her marriage, her infertility, what had he told her in return? Hardly anything. And definitely not the entire truth in what little he had revealed.

An ache settled at the center of her chest. She had told herself he was just a fling, but last night had felt like more and it made the hurt and betrayal all the harder to endure.

Applause broke out as she felt a merciful end to the continued strain of keeping up appearances. She watched as numerous physicians approached Ryan, no doubt congratulating him on a job well done. Perfect, she thought. She had no need to hear any more lies. She gathered her bag and made her way to the door. She had just entered the corridor when she felt herself being pulled into another room. Before she could think she was staring at an empty conference room, empty aside from Ryan.

"Your last name is Dufour?" he demanded more than asked.

She was too taken aback to do anything but answer. "Dufour was my married name."

"Is your ex-husband Kevin Dufour?"

She felt as if she'd been slapped and recoiled. Just hearing Kevin's name on Ryan's lips meshed two realities that she never wanted joined. How did he know Kevin? And what on earth gave him the right to be this angry?

"Yes," she answered defiantly. She wasn't at all proud of that fact but she still was not deserving of whatever was summoning Ryan's anger.

"So you're the one." Ryan ran his fingers through his hair and she had the feeling that he was as disturbed by this conversation as she was. It made no sense to her but she wasn't going to let him continue to attack her.

"I'm the one? The one who lied? No, that would be you."

"I didn't lie to you."

"I consider significant omissions lies, Ryan. Unfortunately I am used to being lied to. I'm just sorry I didn't realize the type of man you were earlier."

His eyes blazed at her as he stepped one step closer to her. "Don't compare him to me."

"Why not?" The realization that Ryan was very familiar with her ex had dawned and she had no problem comparing them in her anger, even when deep down she still sensed that they were very different men. "You are both liars who say what a woman wants to hear, no matter what the truth really is."

"People who live in glass houses shouldn't throw stones."

"What is that supposed to mean?"

"It means I don't believe your victim act. I know the truth."

"The truth about what? What is the truth, Ryan? Do you even know the meaning of the word?"

"I know you had no problem destroying the life of an innocent woman to get what you wanted. You got what you deserved."

She rapidly processed everything he'd just said. *You got what you deserved.* Wasn't that what she had thought when she'd lost her baby? When she couldn't conceive again? It had taken a lot of healing to accept that that wasn't how life worked. She had taken care of enough other infertile women to know that being infertile wasn't the fate of the unworthy.

She was on the verge of leaving this conversation and him before she suffered any more abuse when the rest of his words came through to her: *destroying the life of an innocent woman to get what you wanted.* She thought back to the confrontation she'd had with Kevin's girlfriend after their marriage. She could see the woman perfectly in her mind and the connection became clear. The nose, the eyes, they were the feminine form of Ryan's. "Sabrina…"

"Sabrina Callum, my sister."

Had he known? Had he always known who she was? Was this some sort of revenge for the pain she had caused his sister? Had he seduced her just to hurt her because she had hurt his sister? She blinked hard but when she opened her eyes it was still Ryan and he still looked at her as though she was nothing.

She thought back to her conversation with Sabrina and the pain she had felt on learning for the first time of Kevin's infidelity. To think a part of her had still clung to hope for her marriage. In the end she had been the loser in the love triangle because as much as Sabrina had been hurt by Kevin's betrayal, at least she hadn't had to endure the continual infidelity and emotional abuse Erin had over the years of their marriage.

"She was lucky." She spoke her mind, not meaning to anger him further but also not holding back.

"Lucky?" He seemed stunned.

"Yes, lucky."

"Do you know what you did to her? What it was like for her to one day have the man she loved and had been with for years, the man she was engaged to marry, drop her completely and marry another woman within weeks?"

He was yelling at her now but she couldn't respond. Had she thought about Sabrina—yes, but only after she and Kevin had married because that had been when she'd learned of her. But to be honest she hadn't agonized over the other woman's pain because she had been deep in her own, first learning that her husband had not been faithful and had cast her in the role of the other woman, then struggling with the pain and complications from her miscarriage.

Erin looked up at Ryan and realized there was no point. Nothing was as it seemed. He was no longer a fresh start, an honest man who would renew her faith in men. She honestly didn't know which was worse—the fact that he was a liar or that maybe he had seduced her intentionally to avenge his sister. Either way, it didn't matter. There was no point in arguing further. She didn't care to explain herself to him and there was nothing he could say to her to regain her trust.

"Goodbye, Ryan."

He watched as she walked away from him and tried not to notice that she held her head up. He was still reeling from the sight of her sitting on that panel and the introduction that had been made. As she had been introduced his mind had sparked from one connection to another until the final unfortunate conclusion. Her last name was Dufour, her ex-husband was an orthopedic surgeon and she was from Boston. She was the other woman.

He thought of the glimpses of Sabrina he had seen over the months she had been sick. Serving away, he hadn't been a continuous presence in her life, but even from a distance he had learned enough about the unsavory details of her breakup with Kevin. How he had been entranced and seduced by a woman named Erin, who had then trapped him with a pregnancy, giving him no choice but to leave Sabrina to marry her. Now, having met Erin, he felt torn. Part of him wanted to believe what he had learned of her over their two days together. But the other part of him knew the wickedness of her past actions and worried that she had conned him, as well.

Was he that transparent that she had managed to morph herself into exactly what he wanted? He felt his heart begin to pound at the other possibility. She had trapped one man into marriage, was that her plan again? The sadness she had expressed when she'd told him of her infertility had been so believable he hadn't bothered with a condom again. He was the only kind of fool. Never had he ever trusted a woman when it came to contraception and now there was the possibility of significant consequences for his first lapse in judgment. Time will tell, he thought to himself. He had no doubt that if Erin was pregnant she would make him pay for his mistake.

CHAPTER SIX

Two years later...

"PUSH," SHE ENCOURAGED the woman, whose mind and body spoke of true exhaustion. Erin glanced at the monitor displaying the baby's heart rate.

"Push, Allison. I know you can do this." She kept all sense of panic from her voice as she mentally formulated her backup plan if Allison did not have her baby in the next five minutes.

Another set of pushes and Erin finally saw the progress she had been hoping for. "Perfect, Allison, that's perfect," she encouraged softly.

She would never get tired of this. The experience of watching a couple who at that moment were as close as two people could be welcoming a child into their lives.

"I can't." A small plea escaped from the head of the bed.

"Yes, you can, Allison, and you are. Just a little bit longer and you will get to meet your baby. Now push."

She alternated her attention between the baby's head and the monitor. One-twenty, one hundred, ninety, eighty... The number and the graph descended below normal range.

"Allison." Her eyes were closed and her head tipped back. "Next contraction you need to have the baby."

The woman's eyes opened wide and Erin knew she had gotten through to her. "It's coming," Allison declared.

"Okay, let it build, take a deep breath in, hold it and push."

And a minute later Erin was holding a small, perfect person for just a brief moment before she put him on his mother's chest, gently rubbing him with a towel to stimulate breathing.

She exhaled when a small cry filled the room, followed by his mother's tears of happiness. "Congratulations, momma, you did it."

She finished everything she needed to do and completed her final checks in silence, not wanting to interfere with the couple's moment. After carefully disposing of sharp instruments and counting the sponges, she was ready to leave to complete the required paperwork.

"Congratulations again," she wished them both.

"Thank you so much, Dr. Madden, we couldn't have done it without you."

"Yes, you could have, but thank you for including me." She gave Allison a gentle squeeze on her foot before grabbing the chart.

Erin walked behind the desk on Labor and Delivery and began her charting. She glanced at her watch. It was almost midnight, but it had been worth it. She had followed Allison through her fertility treatments and her pregnancy, and now she had a son. Her pager blared through her peace. She glanced at the number. It was the emergency department.

Instantly her heart began to race, as it always did when she saw those numbers, and she had to concentrate on breathing. She didn't know why she was being paged. She wasn't on call tonight; she had come in on her own time for Allison.

She took a deep breath and let professionalism take precedence over her fear. She dialed the numbers and waited until the call was answered. "It's Erin Madden."

"Dr. Madden, we need you in the emergency department now," the unit clerk relayed to her.

There was nothing normal about the request. Usually she would speak directly with the consulting physician and hear the details of the patient consultation. Never had she been almost ordered to appear.

"What's going on?" She could hear chaos in the background.

"I don't know. Dr. Callum just yelled out that I needed to get you here as soon as possible."

The sense of dread she had been carrying around for the past two years solidified within her. The minute she had seen the announcement welcoming him to Boston General she had been waiting for this moment, but she had almost convinced herself she was going to be able to avoid it indefinitely. As chief resident, she made the schedule and before she assigned herself shifts she always looked at the emergency department schedule to ensure their shifts never aligned. Tonight she wasn't supposed to be here but she was and so was he and he was calling for her.

"Did he say why?" she asked quietly, wondering if Ryan having the unit clerk make the call was his way of making sure she didn't avoid him.

"No, he's tied up trying to stabilize Dr. Darcy."

Erin did a double take as she replayed the clerk's words in her head. "Do you mean work with Dr. Darcy?"

"No. Dr. Darcy was found unconscious in the women's change room. He's with her now."

"I'm on my way."

Erin ran. She rarely ran, but today she ran from the maternity unit to the waiting bank of central elevators. As she frantically pushed the button she tried to control her panic. Chloe. Something was wrong with Chloe and she needed her, and in order to do that she was going to have to see Ryan again.

The minute the doors opened she ran through the halls to the emergency department, going first to the trauma bays, where she feared she would find her. She came to an abrupt halt at the sight before her. Chloe lay on a stretcher, pale and barely conscious of the commotion around her. She was already hooked up to the monitors and Erin glanced at the screen. Her pulse was high at one hundred and fifty. Her blood pressure was low at eighty over forty. She was in shock.

"Where are we at?" she asked the group, needing an answer.

"She's received four units of packed red blood cells and two units of fresh frozen plasma from the rapid transfuser." The voice came from behind her and she didn't need to turn to recognize its owner.

"Can I speak to you alone for a moment, Dr. Madden?"

She could do this, she told herself. She had already been through so much that she could do this, too. She had no choice but to turn and confront the man she had been successfully avoiding until now. "Yes, Dr. Callum."

She watched as recognition flared in his eyes and for a moment he was stunned into silence.

"Dr. Callum, what's wrong with Chloe?" she asked, doing everything possible to bring him back to the professionalism Chloe needed.

"She was found unconscious in the women's change room. A bedside rapid ultrasound of her abdomen reveals a significant amount of free fluid and her beta HCG has returned positive."

She looked away from him back at Chloe. The presentation was classic for one thing, a ruptured ectopic pregnancy, which meant that Chloe was in serious danger and needed her entire focus.

"I need to call the operating room and have them get ready. Make sure she is prepped and ready to go in the next five minutes." She walked away from Ryan toward the nursing desk and one of the phones.

"This is Erin Madden. I have a ruptured ectopic in the emergency department. We need to come now. Set up for an attempted laparoscopic removal and possible laparotomy."

She moved from the phone back to Chloe's side, lifting the hospital gown and feeling her abdomen herself. It was distended and rigid beneath her touch. She pushed down just slightly and heard Chloe moan in response. "It's okay, Chloe. I'm going to take good care of you," she murmured as reassuringly as she could, when inside she was scared to death.

Ectopic pregnancies were still among the highest killers of women in pregnancy. Often they were caught early since women now had more access to ultrasounds in pregnancy and were able to be treated medically. But occasionally they presented without the woman noticing any warning signs and a perfectly healthy woman like Chloe could in an instant be on the brink of death.

She worked through her plan in her head, reminding herself she needed not to do anything differently just because it was her friend. She needed to use the same common surgical sense she would with any other patient. She walked back to the phone and called her supervising staff.

"Hello, it's Thomas."

"Dr. Thomas, it's Erin Madden. I got called to the emergency department for an unstable, probably ruptured ectopic pregnancy that I've just booked for the operating room."

"Erin, you're not on call tonight." The voice was questioning, but not with any misgivings.

"The patient is Dr. Chloe Darcy, the chief resident from Emergency. They called me directly."

"Say no more. I'll meet you in the operating room."

She made two more calls, first to the blood bank to arrange for more blood products to be dropped off directly to the operating room and second to the resident on call to assist. Out of the corner of her eye she saw Chloe being wheeled down the hall toward the elevators for the operating room.

She still needed to change into fresh scrubs, give handover to the awaiting anesthetist and check to make sure the right equipment had been picked, so she took off running. This time she took the single flight of stairs to the second floor, focused only on the task ahead of her. She had half pulled off her scrub top before even entering the change room and quickly completed the task before arriving ready in theater seven.

The anesthetist was at the head of the bed, preparing for Chloe's arrival. "What do you have, Erin?"

"A previously healthy thirty-year-old female with a probable ruptured ectopic pregnancy. She was hypotensive and tachycardic in the emergency department. She has two central large-bore intravenous, each in an antecubital fossa on her arms. She has received four units of packed red blood cells and two of fresh frozen plasma. No repeat CBC has been done yet. I've arranged for another four and two units to be delivered directly to the operating room. I'd like to start laparoscopically."

"Are you sure?"

It was the question she had been asking herself for the past ten minutes. No, she wasn't sure. Starting with the less invasive method might help Chloe in the long run but it also might not work or prolong her time to treatment. Would she be considering this if Chloe were any other patient?

"Yes."

The nursing team brought Chloe into the room and Erin helped transfer her off the bed to the operating table. She watched as the anesthetist did his assessment and felt a small sense of fear grow within her when he called for a second anesthetist to assist him. Erin sat on a stool by Chloe's side, holding the cold hand that lay splayed on the arm board as she was anesthetized, and then it was back to work. Erin positioned Chloe for the planned less invasive surgery before turning to leave the room to complete her surgical scrub in the outside scrub sink. She saw Ryan through the threaded glass windows of the operating-room doors.

She pushed through the doors and he took a few steps back from her. "You need to leave," she stated without anger but with significant conviction.

She understood why he was there. Chloe was loved by everyone and she knew from conversations with her friend that Ryan had become a mentor to her in the emergency department, but still that didn't make a difference to her right now. "Ryan, I can't have any distractions right now. I have a job to do. Think of Chloe."

He seemed to understand. She almost wished she had a minute to look into his eyes and try to figure out what he was thinking, what he was feeling, but she didn't. She checked the ties on her surgical mask and hat before opening the sterile scrub packet and methodically rubbing the sponge up and down each exposed axis of her hands.

When she turned from the sink Ryan was no longer there and she felt a sense of relief, which she knew would only be temporary.

She gowned, gloved and draped Chloe, which made things easier. It helped her separate her fear for her friend from the job she had to do.

"You can start," the anesthetist confirmed.

"Knife." And she held out her hand in anticipation.

Chloe's abdomen was flawless until the moment she made the five-millimeter incision into the base of her belly button. A minute later she had a camera inserted and was staring at the monitor across from her. Chloe's abdomen was a sea of red. She couldn't see anything; particularly she couldn't see where the ectopic was bleeding.

"Can I have her more head down, please?" she asked the anesthetist, hoping that tipping her would move some of the blood away.

"No, I can't move her from where she is now. Her pressure won't tolerate it."

"Okay." She took a deep breath and said the words she didn't want to say. "We are going to convert. Open the laparotomy set."

The nurses in the room scrambled to change the instruments as Erin sterilely repositioned Chloe. "Knife," she called again.

This time her incision was more than five millimeters. She grimaced as she drew the ten-centimeter line just above Chloe's pubic bone, but didn't stop. She worked quickly until she accessed Chloe's abdomen and started removing the blood. She was constantly aware of the amount present as the nurses and anesthetist updated her on the number of canisters she filled and sponges she soaked through. She needed to hurry to stop the bleeding. "Can we make sure that the second four units are on their way?" she directed.

Then she saw it, the continuous pouring from the frayed edges of the ruptured tube. She closed a clamp over it and the bleeding stopped. She felt as if she took her first breath.

"Okay, let's take a moment and finish evacuating all the blood then we'll reassess the tube."

She was buying time. A few minutes later she had to refocus on the Fallopian tube. With the clamp still on she carefully removed the pregnancy from the tube, nothing visible aside from placental tissue and blood clot. Every time she removed a piece the bleeding increased. She struggled in vain to be gentle and not injure the tube further. She tried cautery to burn the edges, but more bleeding ensued. Then she asked for a fine suture for a tension stitch, but the tube was too shredded from the rupture.

"Erin," she heard Dr. Thomas's voice break through her concentration.

"Yes," she answered, already knowing what he was going to say.

"You know what to do." She did. She'd been thinking it for the past five minutes. She nodded in agreement.

"Curved roger." She held her hand out, waiting for the larger clamp. Two steps later she held the Fallopian tube in her hand and felt sick. She hadn't rendered Chloe infertile as she still had her other tube, but still she felt awful about the possibility that Chloe might have difficulty having children in the future.

She looked around again, cleaning things up, until she was aware of a shift in the room. "Do you need help?" It was the voice of Dr. Tate Reed, one of the hospital's most prominent surgeons.

Erin had no idea why Tate was there, but the one thing she was certain of was that she was in control and the only other thing she could do for Chloe was protect her privacy. "You need to leave, Dr. Reed."

"Dr. Thomas?" He was going over her head and Erin held her breath, praying that Dr. Thomas would back her decision.

"Dr. Madden is right. This is not a vascular case, Tate. We are going to have to ask you to leave."

"Okay," Erin heard him concede, but she was also

very aware that he did not venture farther than the operating-theater doors and was watching her every move.

"What is her hemocrit?" she asked, wanting to know if Chloe needed more blood.

She waited as the anesthetist drew a sample and put it in the machine. "Sixty."

"Please give her the next four units and the two fresh frozen plasma."

"If we do, we'll have to keep her warmed and intubated in the intensive care unit."

"She needs the blood. Once she redistributes the rest of her fluid her hemoglobin is going to be much lower than that."

She stared again at where the tube had once been, wanting to be sure Chloe was absolutely dry before she started to close her. The operating-room doors pushed open again. This time she didn't feel any tension at the sight of Chloe's best friend and her friend, Dr. Kate Spence.

"Hi, Kate." Erin acknowledged her presence but didn't change her focus from the surgical pedicles.

"She's going to be okay. We have evacuated the hemoperitoneum and have stopped the bleeding. We are going to be closing in the next few minutes and then she will be going to Recovery, followed by a short stay in the intensive care unit in case she runs into any massive transfusion complications."

"Uh-huh." Kate seemed as stunned as she had been when she'd first got the call. Still, Erin was friends with both women and knew that Chloe was protective of Kate and would want her comforted.

"I'm sorry we had to open her. We tried with the

laparoscope but she had too much blood in her abdomen and was too unstable to tolerate it." She felt self-conscious about her choice, knowing that Kate was a general surgeon with excellent laparoscopic skills.

"But the bleeding has been stopped? Kate asked.

"Yes."

"What happened?" Kate finally asked.

She couldn't answer that. Her job right now was as Chloe's doctor, not Kate's friend. "That's not for me to disclose to you. Chloe will be able to tell you herself later, if she chooses to. I think you should go now and take Dr. Reed with you. She is stable and we'll take good care of her. You can see her in the intensive care unit in a couple of hours, once she's settled in."

"Okay," Kate said, resigned. "Thank you."

Ryan paced the halls of the operating rooms, waiting. His mind flashed with images of the night. Chloe lying lifeless on the change-room floor and all the ways he had seen Erin. First it had been when she had turned around in the emergency department. He hadn't known she'd still been there. Before he had agreed to take a position in the emergency department he had checked the resident listing for the department of obstetrics and gynecology. There were no Dufours listed, or even Erins, for that matter. He had assumed she had left following her divorce and he had taken the job pleased with the knowledge that she was a complication he could avoid.

Then as Chloe had been transferred to the operating room he had assisted and followed her to ensure her well-being. He had seen Erin again, rushing into the change room, her shirt half pulled off before the doors had closed, and that had been when he could no longer have doubts about who he was dealing with. For a moment he had forgotten everything except for the memories of the last time he had shared that intimate a view.

Now he had no choice but to trust Erin with the care of one of his closest friends and he felt absolutely gutted by everything that was happening around him. From the moment he had heard the nurse screaming for help, to holding Chloe unconscious in his arms, realizing that the person he needed to make this right was Erin Dufour, he'd had no control. A career in the military had prepared him for a lack of control, but tonight every coping mechanism had abandoned him. He had already run into Tate Reed in the hallway and lost his temper, something he never did.

The sound of the operating-room doors swinging open got his attention and he looked at Chloe, who was being wheeled out, still intubated, the anesthetist intermittently squeezing oxygen into her. Erin was at the foot of the bed, assisting with the transfer. Her blue eyes met his and she nodded slightly and he knew that Chloe was going to be okay.

After they passed he stood undecided in the hallway until he could resist no longer. He walked into the recovery room and to the desk where Erin sat.

"You're not on the resident list."

Her eyes flashed back at him and he watched as she pulled a blue flowered scrub hat from her head, running her fingers through her hair, which was a darker blond and longer than when he had first met her. "Yes, I am."

"No, you're not. I checked before I came to work here."

She sighed, pulling her nametag from her pocket and laying it before him to read.

"Alexandra Erin Madden," he read aloud.

"My mother's name is Alexandra. I've always gone by Erin."

"And Madden?" he asked, still wondering how he could have not known.

"My maiden name. Sorry to disappoint you." It was a throwaway comment and he knew by both her reaction tonight and the conversation they were having that she was not surprised to see him.

"You knew I was here?"

"Yes," she confirmed.

He thought about all the time he had been at the hospital and realized that he had never seen her. Through his role as an emergency-room attending physician he knew most of the residents across all the programs, which meant one thing. Erin had gone out of her way to avoid him. He had no idea why that angered him, but it did. "You've been avoiding me?"

She stood from her seat and even though she barely cleared his shoulders the effect was still there. "No different than your attempt to avoid me. I was just more successful. If you want to you can pretend you never saw me tonight."

He didn't stop her as she walked away.

Her heart was pounding. She had made it so far and now with less than three months left before her departure from Boston General she had come face-to-face with the one person in the world she had never wanted to see again. She remembered the feeling of betrayal she had felt in Edinburgh and felt uneasy, not knowing who she was dealing with. For the rest of the night she found herself looking over her shoulder, waiting for another encounter with Ryan. She would be a fool to think it wasn't going to happen again. It was just a question of when.

She returned to Labor and Delivery and checked on Allison and then looked at her watch. She had a desperate need to go home and had enough time to do so before Chloe was conscious and ready to talk.

CHAPTER SEVEN

ERIN STOOD OVER the crib and marveled at the miracle it contained. Not one trace of blanket covered the sleeping baby inside. She reached down and pulled the blanket over her again, knowing the action was futile, but it gave her the maternal reassurance she needed right now.

She had thought that seeing Jennie would stem the panic that had started the minute she had seen Ryan, but it had only made it worse. Everyone who had met her little girl had always exclaimed how much she looked like Erin, but only Erin, who was privy to more intimate information, knew how much Jennie actually looked like her father.

She brushed the wisps of brown hair gently, not wanting to disturb the baby but also needing to touch her. If she had woken up, Erin would have had to face Ryan's eyes staring back at her and she wasn't ready to face that reality. How long would it be before he found out about her baby?

She should have left Boston the minute she had heard of Ryan being hired. Certainly the misery of being in the same hospital as Kevin, a torment that had only increased when she'd become pregnant, had been reason enough to leave. But she had needed help. There had been no way she could be a single mother and continue her training in a specialty as demanding as obstetrics and gynecology without the help of her family and friends, so she had stayed.

She hadn't concealed her pregnancy. At the time there had been no reason to, and it was common knowledge she was a single mother. Most people assumed it was her ex-husband's child and that he just regarded the child the same way he had his marriage—with indifference. As much as she didn't like the connection, she had never bothered to correct the assumption. Jennie was the love of her life and she would do anything to protect her miracle.

After some lengthy time had passed, she forced herself to move away from the crib and out of the nursery. It wouldn't be long before her eighteen-month-old daughter would be out of the crib and Erin wanted to hold on to these moments as long as possible.

It had taken her ten positive pregnancy tests even to consider the possibility that she might be pregnant. Stress, she had thought to herself as her cycle had stopped, nausea had begun to rule her life and her abdomen had become uncharacteristically bloated. She'd even thought she might be going crazy, developing symptoms of a phantom pregnancy that she desperately wanted but was never going to have. So she had taken the test to force her unconscious self to face reality and had been completely unprepared for the positive result that had appeared.

She had never heard of a false-positive pregnancy test, so she'd bought another, and another. Then absolute fear had set in when she'd considered the possibility of having a hormone-secreting cancer that had been making the tests positive. It had taken another two weeks of positive tests before she'd forced herself into action and had asked for help from Dr. Thomas, one of her favorite staff obstetricians.

He had been very gentle and kind when he had broken the news of her pregnancy to her. It had been almost laughable that as an obstetrics resident she hadn't diagnosed the obvious, but it had taken so long to accept that she would never have a child that she hadn't allowed herself to even consider the possibility. Even after he'd convinced her that she'd been having a healthy, normal pregnancy she hadn't let herself really believe it.

Every milestone, every change in pregnancy had both amazed and terrified her. Despite the growing contour of her abdomen she'd still had trouble with the reality that she was going to be a mother. It had felt as though if she believed it, it would hurt more if it all went away.

Then one morning she'd gone into labor and as the hours had passed she'd become ever closer to becoming a mother. She had delivered Jennie with her mother by her side and amid the tremendous joy that had flooded her she couldn't help but feel a small amount of sadness that she hadn't had "that moment." The moment that she loved most when delivering babies. The moment when a man looked at the woman he loved, amazed at what she had done and more in love with her than he had ever been. Instead, while holding Jennie, the moment with her baby's father had been a memory of how she had misplaced her trust yet again and the anger and disdain Ryan felt for her.

The moral part of her had thought about finding him, letting him know they had a daughter. But the protective mother in her had said no. She couldn't say she knew Ryan, not after he had made it clear how he felt about her. She'd known enough to know he wouldn't just thank her for the news and move on. He would want Jennie; who wouldn't? And given the feelings he had for her and his view of her as a person there had been the chance that maybe he would even feel that he was the better parent and try to take full custody. That risk was one she had decided she was not willing to take.

Now that question was reopened. It wasn't a secret that she had a daughter. How long could she last before he put together the puzzle?

Her pager buzzed against her hip and she recognized the number as being that of the intensive care unit. Chloe must be awake. She moved back into the nursery, gently pressed her lips to her hand and onto Jennie's cheek before leaving quietly.

Ryan walked to the bank of computer screens and stared at the images. Black-and-white images filled the screens and he searched for the fracture. He knew it was there. There was no way the cyclist's wrist and arm was that swollen and tender without a fracture, but why couldn't he see it? Because he was distracted. Thinking about Erin. His stubborn pride kept him from simply waiting for the radiologist's report and finally after several minutes the subtle thin line became apparent.

He walked back to the nursing desk. "Who's on for Orthopedics?"

"Dufour."

Perfect, thought Ryan, clenching his jaw to keep his teeth from gritting. He hadn't avoided Kevin since coming to Boston but he also hadn't gone out of his way to make contact with him, either. He had never been close with the other man. When Kevin had been engaged to Sabrina he had seen him socially on one or two occasions when he'd had leave from the military. Each time he had seemed charming and the perfect match for his sister. When Sabrina had talked about him it had been nothing but praise and happiness.

Even when their relationship had ended Sabrina had placed minimal blame on Kevin. He had been lured away. Enticed and trapped by another woman. Now he knew that woman was Erin. He had blamed Kevin more, seen him as weak. But that had been before he, too, had fallen for her charms.

After Edinburgh he had struggled for months to reconcile how he felt about Erin. He would replay all of the time they'd spent together, trying to find the crack, the hairline clue that she had been pretending to be something she wasn't. Trying to appeal to everything he wanted in a woman. Had she intentionally thrown herself from the hillside, knowing he would save her? It seemed ridiculous but he felt as if he couldn't put anything past her. Unlike the fracture today, he had never found that crack, and that frustration he'd felt toward her had only increased because of it.

The confrontation after he'd discovered her true identity had been enough, though. Just hearing her acknowledge his sister, what she had done to her and calling her lucky had been enough to make Ryan want to turn his back on her and walk away forever. Now he no longer had that luxury. She was in Boston, at Boston General Hospital, and the past was simply not going to be able to remain just that.

"Please page him," he told the nurse.

A few minutes later she handed him the phone.

"This is Dufour."

"This is Ryan Callum. I have a wrist fracture in Emergency I would like you to see."

"Page my resident." The reply was both arrogant and irritating. If Kevin had any memory of Ryan it wasn't apparent by his tone.

"Your resident is three consultations behind and seeing them between operative cases. We need to clear the backlog in the emergency department."

"That's not my problem," Kevin dismissed.

"I'm making it your problem." It was a tone he didn't use often, but he wasn't in any frame of mind to take any condescension from Kevin Dufour.

"Who is this?"

"Dr. Ryan Callum, staff emergency physician. We've met."

There was no response on the other end of the line. It was almost as if Dufour was searching his memory for when he had met Ryan. "So are you coming to see the patient or should I call another orthopedic surgeon?"

"Be my guest."

"I will. I hear Dr. Williamson is interested in keeping his hand in clinical practice." The conversation could not have gotten more antagonistic. He had known exactly what he was doing, bringing up the chief of staff and Dufour's former father-in-law. The phone clicked and a few seconds later he heard the empty dial tone.

"Is he coming?" the nurse beside him asked. He could tell that by the small uplift of the corner of her mouth that she had heard and approved of his handling of the conversation.

"I think so."

Ryan continued his charting, sure in his assumption. Dufour would come, not immediately but he would come. Thirty minutes later he saw the other man, striding arrogantly toward him. He took in his appearance, which hadn't changed much since their last meeting, his all-American pretty-boy good looks still at their finest.

"Just exactly who do you think you are?" Apparently their conversation was not over.

"At this moment I'm the senior staff physician responsible for the emergency department."

"Let me make something clear—you don't tell me what to do."

Ryan smirked slightly. It was almost comical watching Dufour make an attempt to intimidate him. He had spent over a decade in the military, including combat experience, surrounded by superiors who had been the essence of intimidation and fellow soldiers who had all been volleying for promotion. Dufour's obvious peacocking was nothing to him, except that it once again challenged his past perceptions of the other man. He was nothing like the charmer Ryan had once met. And with his attempt at dominance neither was he the weak man he had envisioned being seduced by Erin.

Erin. Despite the fact that he couldn't claim to

know her, not really given what he knew about her past and the facade she had presented in Edinburgh, he still couldn't picture her with this man. Never mind be married to him.

"The patient is in exam six." And he walked away, having heard enough from Dufour. He came to a dead stop when the idea in his mind penetrated his thoughts. Sabrina was lucky not to have married him. He thought of her life now. She had since married, had a son and settled down for a quiet life in the suburbs that she loved. Discomfort tore through him when he realized he was thinking exactly what Erin had said to him. When she'd said it he had been furious. But, still, even if that was the case, Erin hadn't known that back then. Not when she'd been seducing another woman's fiancé. But after a few moments with Kevin he was certain that Sabrina had had a lucky escape. But had Erin gotten what she'd deserved?

Erin felt exhausted as she finished her clinic day. Infertility work was 10 percent happiness and 90 percent emotionally draining. Talking to couples about their options, none of which had any guarantee, was a hard conversation. Then there was Chloe.

She had followed up on her twice daily in hospital. Their first conversation had been very hard. Telling her friend that she had been pregnant and had then lost the pregnancy had brought back old memories of the feelings she'd had when she had been in Chloe's position. That feeling of "Why me" and all the possible answers to that question. She had done her best to be Chloe's friend but also remain professional, when truthfully all she'd wanted to do had been to cry along with her.

Now she was busy juggling the demands of her regular work, taking care of Chloe and living with the constant threat of Ryan discovering her secret.

She drew in her breath as she saw him. She wasn't surprised to see him—she'd known it was inevitable. There was no way she could turn around and walk away; she didn't want him to think she had anything to hide. Besides, other than their daughter, she had nothing to hide from him and nothing to be ashamed of. He had accused her of immoral behavior when she had been nothing but honest about her life and past with him. She hadn't even lied by omission, not then, because she'd had no idea Ryan was connected with her past. Now she had no choice. She would lie. She was going to do everything she needed to do to protect her family.

They met outside Chloe's door at the same time.

"Ryan."

"Erin. You're here to see Chloe?"

"She's my patient," she replied, hating that she felt a need to defend herself against such a simple question.

"She's my friend."

"Mine, too."

"Chloe never mentioned you." He was staring at her with suspicion in his eyes.

"Why would she?" She knew he was getting at something and felt a need to emotionally brace herself.

"Did you tell her?"

"About?"

"Scotland."

Chloe had asked about Erin's romantic Scottish

love affair when she had returned home and without
giving any details Erin had been firm about not wanting to discuss it and Chloe had been gracious enough
to not ask anything further. As far as Erin knew, she
had never put together that the Ryan Callum in the
emergency department was the same military Ryan
Erin had met in Scotland.

"No, I didn't. Enough of my mistakes are public
knowledge. I didn't think my latest poor choice in
men was worth mentioning." She knew she shouldn't
antagonize him, but now, outside the life-and-death
scenario Chloe had presented, all of the hurt she had
felt as a result of Ryan had come flooding back.

"It probably would have been difficult to explain
that you passed yourself off as something you were
not and then the truth came out."

"Are you talking about me or you?" She pushed
past him and into Chloe's room. She didn't make it
far. Chloe's room was filled with their friend Kate and
Dr. Tate Reed. She remembered how she'd had to be
firm with Tate in the operating room and had asked
him to leave. She hoped he realized she had done
what had been best for Chloe and wasn't angry with
her, because she didn't need another confrontation
right now.

"I just came to see if you needed anything," Erin
said, deciding to focus on the only person who mattered in the room—her patient.

"I'm good, thank you." She still looked tired and
wary but, considering how she had looked a few days
earlier, Erin would take it.

"When do you think Chloe will be discharged?"
Tate asked, his entire attention focused on her. She

quickly glanced at Chloe, who didn't object to Tate's question and appeared to be waiting for the answer.

"She can be discharged tomorrow if she feels well enough to go. But she can't stay alone for the first few weeks."

"She can stay with me," Kate volunteered.

Erin had assumed that was what would happen so hadn't addressed discharge planning with Chloe prior to this conversation. She was shocked when Chloe declined the offer. She was about to offer her own home when Ryan interrupted her.

"Chloe, you are welcome to stay with me." His offer rang with confidence. Erin looked back at him, stunned by his offer. Chloe had never mentioned anything beyond a professional mentor-mentee relationship between them. She knew they were close professionally but not personally. Their lack of personal relationship outside the hospital had provided comfort to Erin, knowing there wasn't a possibility she see Ryan socially through her friendship with Chloe.

"I don't think that's a good idea," Tate replied, before anyone else could interject. Erin was forced to look at both men and the same feeling she had gotten the other night from Tate returned. He obviously cared very much about Chloe and she felt a small twinge of pain at what she didn't have.

She was lost in her own thoughts so that it wasn't until she heard Kate's and Chloe's simultaneous gasps that she realized the conversation had escalated and it felt as though Tate and Ryan could come to blows at any moment.

"I agree with Tate," Erin interrupted the men's discussion. She wasn't sure exactly what had been said, but she knew from personal experience that staying with Ryan was not in Chloe's best interests. All eyes turned to her.

"I don't think *you* are the right person to comment on propriety," Ryan rebuked.

She heard the gasps again, and she would have gasped, too, if she'd had any higher expectations of Ryan's opinion of her, but she didn't. If anything, it reinforced her decision to keep the knowledge of Jennie to herself.

"*Enough.* I appreciate everyone's concern, but I am an adult, capable of making my own decisions and deciding what is in my own best interests. Erin, are you sure I can't go back to my apartment as long as I don't overdo it?" Thank goodness for Chloe. Erin did her best to let go of Ryan's barb before turning back to her patient.

"Yes, I'm sure. With your low hemoglobin and naturally low blood pressure I think you are at high risk for dizziness and fainting and you shouldn't be alone." There, she had done what she had come to do, take care of Chloe. It was decided that Chloe would go and stay at Tate's and, to be honest, Erin was pleased. Tate was a good man. He cared for her, and maybe, just maybe, her recovery would bring them both together. Just because she was unlucky in love, it didn't mean that her friend couldn't find happiness.

She casually said her goodbyes and left the room, trying to make her escape without it being obvious.

"Erin."

She heard Ryan call out her name before she had made it a few feet from the door. She knew she had no choice but to stop for fear that their pending conversation became even more public than it was about to be.

"Ryan," she acknowledged, as she turned and watched as he quickly made up the distance between them.

"What did you think you were doing in there?" It wasn't hard to read the anger in his voice.

"Being insulted in front of my patient and my friends," she replied, before she could stop herself. What was it about Ryan that made her speak her mind and her feelings so freely?

Her words seemed to penetrate through him and the tension between them lowered. "I'm sorry."

At that moment she was more shocked than she had been in Chloe's room. She had been expecting an attack, anger, not the return of the Ryan she thought she'd once known, albeit briefly. "Thank you." She accepted his apology as best she could. "It wasn't about you. I think Chloe would be better off with Tate personally and professionally. It would hurt her professional reputation if she moved in with one of her staff physicians, no matter what the reason. Tate has nothing to do with her career."

She hoped he accepted her explanation and they were done talking. It hurt more than she would have liked it to—to be reminded of how perfect she had thought he was in Edinburgh.

"I talked with your ex-husband this morning." She was acutely aware of him waiting for her reaction to his statement.

"And…"

"And what?"

"There is something you are either waiting to say

or are not saying. Either way, I have nothing to do with Kevin and am not responsible for his behavior, past or present. Are we done here?"

He paused and she could feel his visual assessment of her. The black pencil skirt and turquoise blouse she had chosen now felt more revealing than it had looked in the mirror that morning. She tucked her hair behind her ear before looking him in the eye with raised brows.

"You were right about Sabrina being lucky," he confessed.

Before she could respond to what had almost sounded like an apology, he walked away from her.

CHAPTER EIGHT

ERIN WALKED THROUGH the emergency department with her normal sense of unease heightened. She hadn't had time to check who the attending emergency physician was. She was still counting the days until she was done at Boston General and holding her breath that her secret would remain hidden from Ryan.

As the chief resident, Erin ran her own clinic, filled with patients she took primary responsibility for. Tara, an infertility patient, had called that morning with all the classic symptoms of hyperstimulation syndrome, a condition in which as a result of fertility treatments, overstimulated ovaries caused excess fluid all over the body. Normally she would see all her patients in clinic, well away from Ryan in the emergency department, but Tara had sounded sick on the phone and Erin was worried she was going to need to be more closely monitored.

That morning she had chosen a fitted, knee-length yellow dress with a boat neck, which she had paired with her favorite string of black beads and black slingback low-rise heels. It was perfect for clinic, but she looked and felt out of place in the emergency department.

"Has Tara Compton arrived yet?" she asked the main unit clerk.

"Yes, Dr. Madden, she's in treatment room four."

Erin's assessment had been right. If Tara's symptoms had been mild she would have been placed in one of the lesser acuity rooms. She shook her head. She shouldn't have triggered her ovaries and done the retrieval. She had known throughout Tara's treatment cycle that this was a risk. Her ovaries had responded too well to the medication she'd received and had swelled beyond normal size. But Tara had begged her. Her husband had severe infertility problems and in vitro fertilization had been their only hope of pregnancy. They had saved for five years and this cycle was their only shot at a family. So Erin had persisted and performed the egg retrieval earlier in the week, doing everything she could to lower the risk, but it hadn't been enough.

She walked into the room and struggled to keep her feelings inside. Tara looked very unwell, sitting upright in bed and leaning forward as she struggled to catch her breath. Her abdomen was visibly swollen, so much so that she already looked six months pregnant. Erin glanced at the monitor screen displaying her patient's vitals. Tara's blood pressure was low and her respiratory and heart rates were both above normal.

"Hi, Tara," she greeted her, trying to keep any sense of alarm from her voice.

"Dr. Madden, I don't feel well." Erin noticed that she sounded breathless trying to complete the simple sentence.

"I know," Erin empathized. She already knew Tara

and her history well, so she directed her attention to the immediate problem. "When did this start?"

"Yesterday."

"What is bothering you most?"

"I can't seem to catch my breath and my stomach is hard and swollen."

Erin listened to her chest, noting the decreased breath sound at her lung bases. She tapped her fingers on the base of the lung fields, noting the fullness. With the help of Tara's husband she lowered her onto her back. "I won't keep you here long," she reassured her, aware of the panic in her patient's eyes.

She placed her hands on Tara's abdomen. Uncovered, it looked worse, and Erin estimated there were at least five liters of fluid present. She was able to feel the shift of fluid against her hand as she pushed on one side. With care she helped Tara up again, trying to ease her labored breathing.

She peeked out of the room's curtain and got the attention of one of the nurses assigned to the treatment area. "We need to get some bloodwork and a chest X-ray, stat."

"What would you like, Dr. Madden?"

"Complete blood count, electrolytes, creatinine, prothombin time, prolonged prothombin time, liver enzymes and three views of the chest. Once the blood is drawn and X-ray is done, we are going to set up for an abdominal paracentesis and bedside ultrasound." She held her breath for a moment. "Who is the attending physician in Emergency today?"

"Dr. Callum is on until four this afternoon."

It wasn't what she wanted to hear, but she had few other options.

"Thank you."

She went back into the treatment room to explain the plan to Tara and her husband and then went in search of Ryan. She didn't have to look for long before she found him. He was standing at the physicians' desk, charting.

"Dr. Callum," she addressed him, her only goal to keep this conversation professional.

She saw the muscles in his back and shoulders tense before he turned to meet her eye. She couldn't help but notice how the dark navy of his hospital scrubs complemented his eyes.

"Erin, you can call me Ryan."

"I need your help with a patient."

"What do you have?"

"A twenty-eight-year-old woman with severe ovarian hyperstimulation syndrome She has significant ascites and I need help with a paracentesis."

"What do you need me for?"

"I can't do the procedure blind. I can't risk accidentally puncturing one of the ovaries. I need another physician to do a simultaneous bedside ultrasound so that I can see where I'm going."

"Okay, call me when you're set up and ready."

Thirty minutes later she reviewed all the results and made plans to admit Tara to hospital. She had ordered supplemental oxygen and intravenous fluids to make up for the fluids that were accumulating in her abdomen. She had all the supplies ready and she asked the nurse to get Ryan.

He walked into the room and took his place on the opposite side of the bed from her. "Hi, I'm Dr. Callum. I'm going to be assisting Dr. Madden with the procedure."

Erin wasn't sure why, but the anxiety reaction she had felt for the past two years with regard to Ryan didn't reappear. In fact, the trepidation she had over the upcoming procedure was dissipating. "Okay, Tara, I'm just going to wash your abdomen with this sterile solution. It's really important you keep your hands by your sides and not touch any of the drapes I'm going to cover you with."

She performed the described actions and then looked at Ryan, who nodded his understanding. With the ultrasound probe sterilely draped, he scanned her abdomen. Erin interpreted the black-and-white images on the screen for both Ryan's and Tara's benefit. She could see the black of the accumulated fluid and the outlines of the enlarged ovaries.

"Can you measure the ovarian cysts, please?"

She watched as he did what she asked. "The left side is twelve centimeters and the right side is ten centimeters."

"Thank you."

"Is that big?" Tara asked, an obvious look of fear present in her eyes.

"It meets the criteria for severe," Erin answered. "Now you are going to feel the small burn of the freezing before I do the poke to drain the fluid. Dr. Callum, can you stay centered on the pocket on the left?"

"Yes."

With a precise and quick motion she inserted the needle into Tara's abdomen, quickly enough to limit the discomfort but slowly enough that she could see the opacity of the tip of the needle as it appeared on the screen. As soon as she confirmed placement she removed the sharp tip, leaving the thin plastic catheter that had overlain the needle, and set up the tubing to the suction canisters. She was rewarded as straw-colored fluid began to drain. Then all there was to do was to sit at the bedside and wait.

"Dr. Madden," Tara's voice interrupted her thoughts.

"Yes?"

"Are we still going to be able to do the transfer?" Tara asked, though her tone made Erin believe she already suspected the answer to the question.

"No, we can't. You are pretty sick right now. If we put your fertilized embryos back, it is only going to worsen your condition."

Tears filled the other woman's eyes and began to fall down her face. "I don't care about me. I want a baby." It was an explanation Erin understood perfectly.

Holding the catheter, she contaminated her other hand by taking Tara's. "You will have a baby. It's just going to take a little more time. We'll freeze these embryos and when you are better and ready we'll transfer them back. The most important person to a baby is its mama, and we need to think of you first."

"Are you sure?"

"Yes, I'm one hundred percent sure."

It took twenty minutes, but eventually Erin had removed the bulk of the fluid. Afterward Tara was able to breathe more easily and appeared much more comfortable. She still needed to remain in hospital, but with supportive care was on her way to recovery.

"Thank you, Dr. Callum," Erin said to Ryan, as she pulled the catheter. He nodded at her and left.

She stayed with Tara for a while longer, reviewing her plan for her hospitalization and also her future fertility treatments.

"You were good in there." Ryan's voice met her as she left the room.

"Thank you."

"I think we need to talk."

"I thought you had said everything you needed to say to me in Scotland." She needed him to know that he had hurt her and she wasn't prepared to let it happen again.

"Meet me at five in the lobby?"

She felt lost for words to respond to his request and he took her silence as acceptance as he walked away from her and back to work.

She couldn't believe it herself as she strolled into the lobby of Boston General. She had tried to talk herself out of meeting Ryan but hadn't been able to do it. She felt as though she owed him something, her guilt over keeping Jennie a secret from him growing with every kind word and reminder of the man she had once thought he was. But she still couldn't get past the way they had ended in Scotland. The one-hundred-and-eighty-degree turn from the man he had been had left her lost for how to feel about him. She had memories of the time they had spent together before the symposium, but everything that was happy in her mind had been colored by what had come after.

She saw him sitting in a chair by the large glass wall that defined the atrium's entrance. He had changed and for the first time since she had seen him the night of Chloe's collapse he was not in scrubs.

She stopped halfway to him and let her mind process the effect, and at that moment he turned and it was completed. It was the same man she had been with in Scotland and she had to mentally give herself a shake to remind her that he actually wasn't. She couldn't move from her spot as she watched him come to her.

"Let's get out of here."

She needed time to sort herself out so she mutely followed him.

Ten minutes later she slid into a booth at a wine bar a few blocks from the hospital. It wasn't the Irish pub frequented by most of the hospital staff and Erin was grateful for the privacy. They both ordered from the server and again Erin was reminded of their night in Edinburgh and she couldn't help but feel the difference at the jarring discomfort she was feeling at that moment from the ease of that long-ago night.

"I thought we should say what we need to say to each other, as it seems we are going to be working together," Ryan opened.

"You have more you want to say?" Erin asked, still feeling intensely defensive from his previous attack on her.

He drew in his breath and seemed to put her comment aside. "I was surprised to learn who you were in Edinburgh. I didn't handle it well."

"How should you have handled it?" Why was she waiting for a certain response?

"I should have just walked away. I shouldn't have waged a personal attack on you."

So he hadn't known who she was. A sense of relief passed through her but she still couldn't get past his words. It felt like the classic feedback you got in medical school, a good comment mixed with the bad. Funny how, despite the good, she always focused on the negative part. "But you still would have walked away?"

"Yes." There was no hesitation in his response.

"Why?" It was the question she had asked herself after her anger toward him had left enough room for other emotions.

"I can't be with a woman like you."

"Like me?" She knew she was prying words out of his mouth that he didn't want to say, but she hadn't opened this door, he had.

He took a sip from his beer before he looked her in the eye. "A woman who is willing to be the other woman."

Part of her wanted to tell him her side. That she'd had no knowledge of his sister until she'd already been trapped on a path she had never intended. But it bothered her both that she wanted him to think better of her and that she had to defend herself. In the end what had happened between them hadn't all been about her. "You were not entirely honest with me."

"Yes. I'm sorry"

"Why?"

"At the time I had no idea how important it would be."

She wanted to tell him how much she valued honesty. How it was the most important thing to her, but she couldn't take that stand now when she knew she was prepared to lie about their daughter. "You are walking on a slippery slope."

"I know. That's my punishment."

"I don't see how that is a punishment."

"You're making it hard to stand my ground. Even now, just sitting here talking to you, I have to constantly remind myself of the pain you caused my sister."

"And if you don't?"

"If I don't all I see is the woman I met in Scotland who seemed so perfect and with whom I spent the best night of my adult life."

She felt heat rise through her body and she pulled at the neck of her dress before stopping the telling movement and instead reaching for a large sip from her chilled white wine. Ryan felt the same way about that night as she did. What would happen if she did explain her past with Kevin?

When she looked up he was staring at her and she felt lost in the blue of his eyes. As if it were a different time, he reached out, his hand covering hers. "But it is a different time and we are different people, Erin. No woman, no matter how tempting, would ever lead me to betray my sister."

And just like that his hand was gone and she felt the loss as intensely as she had in Scotland. The thoughts of telling him the truth about her past and the truth about her present evaporated. He had just told her that, no matter what, she would never have a place in his life, his family, and she wasn't prepared to take the risk of her daughter being taken to a family she would be excluded from.

"You don't have to worry for long. Temptation has less than two months left at Boston General and then I'm moving for a fellowship in California with no plans to return."

"You don't have to move because of me."

How could he not understand? "I have to move precisely because of people like you. I'm not going to let the mistake of my marriage to Kevin ruin the rest of my life. Thank you for the drink."

She rose from the booth and left the restaurant, not wanting to hear any more. She was a few meters from the restaurant's door when she heard him call her name and she stopped. She felt his hand on her shoulder and she turned toward him. She didn't even recognize his intention before his mouth was on hers and her face was being cradled between his hands. While the kiss started hard and passionate, it progressed to a tender touch before his lips left hers.

"I'm not sure what we were, but I still felt we deserved a proper goodbye."

She looked up at him, wondering if it was worth the risk, hoping they had another outcome, but then panicked. No man was more important than her daughter. "Goodbye," she said, and with strength she hadn't known she had she walked away from him.

CHAPTER NINE

"DR. CALLUM."

Ryan looked up from the chart he had been completing. Amanda, the triage nurse for the evening shift, was standing in front of him.

"Emergency Medical Services has just brought in an eleven-year-old girl with ten out of ten abdominal pain. She's tachycardic, but stable, but overall looks really distressed. I've put her in treatment room two and I was hoping you could see her as soon as possible yourself."

It wasn't often he got requests like these. He normally gave the medical student or resident he was working with the opportunity to see the patient first then review his or her findings. He could tell, though, that Amanda was really worried, and he knew that she didn't worry often.

"I'll see her right now."

He walked the short distance to the treatment area and to room two. He opened the door to find what Amanda had described: an eleven-year-old girl, crying, her whole body rigid in an attempt not to move.

"Hello, I'm Dr. Ryan Callum, the staff emergency

physician on this evening." He introduced himself as he shook hands with each of the girl's worried parents.

"What's your name?" he asked the girl.

"Lauren."

He could tell she was trying to be grown-up and answer his questions.

"Okay, Lauren, when did your stomach start to hurt?"

"At gymnastics," she answered.

He had already come to that conclusion judging by the leotard she was wearing.

"Did you have any pain before gymnastics?"

"No, it came on all of a sudden when I dismounted from the balance beam."

"Okay," he tried to soothe her, "have you ever had pain like this before?"

"No, but it hurts so bad." She started to sob and the minute the cry racked her body she sobbed harder with the movement, perpetuating a painful cycle.

"Does she have any allergies?" he asked her parents.

"No," they both answered.

"How much does she weigh?"

"She's about seventy-five pounds," her mother responded immediately.

"I'll be right back." Ryan walked to the drug room, using his security card to log in to the automated system. He selected Lauren from the list of registered patients and then typed in her weight, as she was a pediatric patient who required all her medication adjusted for her size. He selected the painkiller and waited as the correct drawer was unlocked before withdrawing the medication.

"Okay, Lauren, I'm going to give you some medication to help make you feel better." He waited to see her reaction and was worried when she didn't question the needle he was holding. Most children wouldn't agree to a needle for anything, so the fact that she was ambivalent was a sign of just how much pain the young girl was in. He injected the medication slowly through her intravenous line so she wouldn't have to feel any discomfort with the injection. He waited until he saw her face relax to know the medication had taken effect.

"Lauren, does it hurt more to move or to stay still?"

"Move."

"Can you point to me where you feel the most pain?"

With the most careful movement he had ever seen she moved her hand, not disturbing the rest of her body, and pointed to her lower left side. "I think I'm going to be sick." With a grimace of pain spreading across her face, she rolled to her side. He managed to move quickly for a plastic basin before she vomited.

He helped support her weight and when she was done gently rolled her onto her back, leaving her to rest before redirecting his attention on her parents.

"Does she have any medical problems?"

"No," her mother answered quickly, clearly alarmed by the state of her daughter.

"Any surgeries in the past? Does she take any medications?"

"No, she's always been a very healthy little girl." He could see tears of fear starting to well up in her eyes.

He nodded in acknowledgment and carefully uncovered the girl's abdomen. He touched the upper right half, as far from the spot she had indicated as he could. Her stomach was as rigid as her posture, and she flinched when he palpated gently, but jumped and cried out when he let go.

"It's going to be okay, Mrs. Connor. Lauren is right where she needs to be. I'm going to order a few tests, including an ultrasound, and we will keep on top of her pain and nausea medication so that we can get her as comfortable as possible. Please don't give her anything to eat or drink until I tell you it's okay."

He walked out of the room and found the attending nurse. He glanced at the clock before picking up the phone and dialing the hospital switchboard. "It's Dr. Callum from Emergency. Can you please page the chief resident from General Surgery urgently for me."

"Yes, Dr. Callum. Do you want to stay on the line?"

"Yes."

Two minutes later. "This is Dr. Kate Spence."

"Kate, it's Ryan Callum from Emergency. I have a healthy eleven-year-old girl with a surgical abdomen following sudden onset left lower quadrant pain. She's stable and we are starting with investigations now, but I wanted you to know before you went home for the evening."

"Thanks for the heads-up. I'll be down shortly."

Ryan paced the emergency department, checking on his active patients and waiting for Lauren's results to come in. Kate Spence had come and gone. She agreed with his assessment but wanted to wait for more information before rushing to the operating room.

"Ryan." Erin's voice cut through his thoughts of the girl and started a new one—how was it possible that she had avoided him for so long when now it felt as if their careers were throwing them together at every chance it got? She was wearing scrubs, her hair pulled back and covered by a scrub hat made with purple fabric.

"Kate called me. All pediatric consultations go direct to the chief resident. The scan of Lauren Connor's abdomen shows classic signs of ovarian torsion. She has a left-sided eight-centimeter cyst that has twisted on itself, cutting off blood supply to the ovary and causing it to swell. I'm going to go and talk to her parents and get consent for the operating room. I thought you should know."

"I'll come with you."

She didn't object and he followed her toward Lauren's room. Both parents stood as they entered. Lauren was still lying still, her eyes closed, with occasional moans of pain.

"Mr. and Mrs. Connor, I'm Dr. Madden, the chief resident from Gynecology. The CT scan of your daughter's abdomen shows that her left ovary has become twisted on itself, cutting off its blood supply. She's having pain because it can't drain or receive fresh blood. We need to take her to the operating room and fix it."

"Are you going to take out her ovary?" Mrs. Connor asked, her horror at the idea obvious.

"No. In a child Lauren's age we often untwist it and hope that it heals. If possible we can try to tack the ovary to reduce her risk of it happening again, but we won't proceed with anything that may compromise the health of the ovary."

Ryan alternated his gaze between Lauren, her parents and Erin. He found her words reassuring and his worry for Lauren dissipated. He knew that Erin would do everything she could to save the ovary, the same way she had struggled to save Chloe's Fallopian tube.

"What are we looking at for her recovery?" Mr. Connor asked.

"Hopefully two days in hospital and then a couple of weeks. We are going to try to get her surgery done using a camera and a few incisions that are all less than one centimeter. It will make her postoperative pain a lot less and she will have barely noticeable scars."

"Are you doing it?" the mother asked.

"Yes," Erin answered definitively.

"Good."

Erin crossed the room toward the head of Lauren's bed. "Lauren, I'm not sure how much you heard of what your parents and I just talked about. You're going to come with me and have a nap and while you're sleeping I'm going to take away the pain and make you feel better." She gently reached out and rested her hand on the girl's shoulder for a few moments before walking away.

"She'll be going to the operating room within the hour. There's a family waiting room outside the operating room and she'll go to the pediatric area of the recovery room so that you both can come in and see her as soon as possible."

"Are you a mother, Dr. Madden?" Ryan's attention rocketed to Erin. It was an innocent question. He was often asked if he was a parent when he was treating children, but he knew that for Erin it was a painful one. He looked over at her and she looked absolutely stricken by the question, her pallor evident against the dark blue of her scrubs, her eyes wide.

"Dr. Madden is an excellent surgeon. You're lucky to have her involved in Lauren's care. Dr. Madden, I'll help get Lauren ready for the operation if you want to go upstairs and organize the operating room."

He wasn't expecting a look of gratitude, but Erin just stared at him questioningly before she returned to her planned course of action.

"I'll see you both soon." And she left the room.

Erin exhaled for what felt like the first time since she'd met Lauren Connor. The young girl was slowly waking in the recovery room and the surgery had been a success. She had untwisted the dark swollen ovary and had waited patiently until she'd seen some evidence that the blood vessels feeding it were going to be able to restore it. Before the case she had called home to talk to Jennie's nanny and if she hurried she would still be able to give Jennie her bath and put her to bed.

"How did it go?" She turned and saw Ryan on the other side of the counter she was sitting at. His deflection of Mrs. Connor's question had taken her aback, both by his gallantry and by the guilt that had overcome her when her lie to him had come too close to the surface.

"Great. We did everything laparoscopically and I think the ovary will heal normally. We left the cyst and will follow her closely until it resolves. She's resting comfortably in the pediatric area if you want to see her." She hoped he would as she didn't feel she could face him much longer, knowing her secret.

"You would have been a good mother."

Her mouth felt completely dry as she watched Ryan walk away toward Lauren. She didn't like deceiving him and her doubts in herself were growing by the minute. It was easier when he was judging her, declaring her a lesser and immoral person. Now he was supportive and still attracted to her, she was at a complete loss at how to deal with all the feelings she had toward him. Was she still attracted to him? Yes. The kiss outside the restaurant had left no room for doubt. She also respected him—it was hard not to, knowing his professional reputation and having watched him take care of Chloe and his other patients. But above everything else she was still hurt by him. Hurt that he couldn't see the truth about who she was and that he thought the worst of her. Was she so hurt that she was keeping Jennie from him to hurt him, too? No, she had told herself and reminded herself again.

Erin looked down at her pager and dialed the number.

"Erin, it's Dr. Thomas. If you have a minute I'd like you to come see your friend Chloe in follow-up."

"Is everything okay?" It didn't make sense to her that she would be called for what should be a routine follow-up.

"Just come."

She headed directly to the hospital's outpatient clinic space. Dr. Thomas simply handed her the chart with Chloe's most recent bloodwork on the front page. "It would be a great case for your upcoming board exams. She's in exam room three. Why don't you go see her and do a bedside ultrasound and let me know?"

She nodded in agreement, still not believing what she was reading. She needed to calm herself before she panicked Chloe. She knocked on the door and waited a minute before letting herself in.

"Hey, Chloe. Dr. Thomas paged me to let me know you were in for your follow-up and asked me to come see you. It's hard to believe it has already been six weeks. How are you feeling?"

Chloe was sitting on the exam table, the paper drape drawn over her lap, looking tired but still considerably better than the last time Erin had seen her.

"Okay. Good days and bad days, I guess. I went back to work this week and that has helped. But I haven't been studying nearly as much as I planned and will be more than happy when this exam is done. I'm surprised to see you still at work. I would have thought you would have been off studying, too."

"You know what they say about the best intentions."

"Well, I'm here, aren't I?" She heard the sadness in Chloe's voice and recognized it as the same she had felt after her own miscarriage.

"How are you feeling *really*?" Erin asked, pulling the stool from the end of the bed so she could sit and talk to her friend.

"Disappointed, frustrated—take your pick. It's hard to admit that I made such a mistake, both in getting pregnant and then not even having the medical sense to realize it. I want to be able to move past it, but I can't seem to get back to normal. I still feel tired, nauseated, and I have no control over my emotions, which just leads to more frustration."

Erin looked down again at the bloodwork results. "You may be being slightly hard on yourself."

"I know."

"Chloe, would it be okay if I examined your abdomen and we did a quick bedside ultrasound?" She tried to be reassuring but knew that Chloe knew enough to know that this was not routine.

"Of course. What are you not saying, Erin?"

Erin couldn't answer. Instead she was trying to convince herself that she wasn't feeling what she was feeling. The elevation of Chloe's uterus two centimeters above her pubic bone was consistent with a fourteen-week pregnancy.

"Your bloodwork from this morning shows a persistently elevated beta HCG."

"What does that mean?" Chloe was as confused as Erin had been when she had seen the result.

"It shouldn't still be elevated. If we had performed a salpingostomy and removed only the ectopic pregnancy then some residual placenta might be present in the Fallopian tube, leading to the elevated hormone level, but…"

"But?"

"But your tube had ruptured and we were unable to control the bleeding from the rupture site, so we performed an open right salpingectomy, removing the entire Fallopian tube. The pathology report confirmed the presence of the pregnancy. So your beta HCG shouldn't still be elevated, unless…" She couldn't believe she was about to say this.

"Unless what?"

"Chloe, you may not be able to move on. I think you are still pregnant."

"I don't understand."

"I think your pregnancy was a heterotopic pregnancy. One inside the Fallopian tube and one in the uterus. It's a rare condition, occurring in only one in every five to thirty thousand pregnancies." She wasn't sure who was in more shock, her or Chloe.

"How do we find out for sure?" Chloe asked.

"We look."

And without further discussion Erin squeezed warmed jelly onto Chloe's abdomen and placed the ultrasound probe against her. She saw everything instantly. The uterus filled with amniotic fluid and inside a baby.

"A baby…" Chloe stated with awe.

"Your baby," Erin confirmed. "I'm just going to do some measurements to date the pregnancy."

"There is only one date possible."

Erin smiled as she went along her routine, measuring the baby's head, abdomen and thigh to estimate the gestational age.

"Which makes you about fourteen weeks along."

"Does everything look okay?" Chloe asked.

Erin thought through the complexity of Chloe's case, the heterotopic pregnancy and the complications and medications involved in her initial surgery. Dr. Thomas was right, she was like a hard board exam question. Still, her job wasn't to get lost in the academics; she needed to focus on supporting Chloe.

"As much as I can see right now, everything looks okay, but we're going to need to do some investigations. You received a lot of blood products that they initially didn't have time to match against your own blood screen. You also received some medication we don't recommend in pregnancy, but right now you have a baby."

"A baby…"

"How do you feel about that, Chloe?"

They both turned to watch the monitor and the baby's activity. Erin remembered when she had first seen Jennie and how special it had been to hear her heartbeat for the first time. She moved the ultrasound cursor over the baby's heartbeat and the rapid sound filled the room.

"Wonderful."

"Okay, so we will just go from here. I am going to give you a requisition for prenatal bloodwork and another ultrasound in four weeks' time so we can look at the rest of the baby's anatomy."

"Erin, is it weird that I am excited and terrified at the same time?"

Erin thought back to when she had finally realized she was pregnant with Jennie.

"No, I remember that feeling well. You're going to be a wonderful mother, Chloe. Congratulations."

CHAPTER TEN

A WEEK OF sleepless nights had done nothing to strengthen Ryan's resolve. He hadn't seen Erin since she had taken care of Lauren Connor, but she still filled his waking thoughts and his dreams. He struggled with his feelings toward her.

Watching her take care of the young girl had shown another side of her he had never seen. Amid her professional behavior she had also managed to show her maternal side. It was one more part of her he found disarming. If everything he knew about her was true, it was as though her pros and cons were balancing on a scale and was worried that any minute the scale might tip to the positive side and he would be forced to choose between Erin and his sister.

If he had never learned about her past with Kevin he would be doing everything in his power to make her his, forever. But he couldn't live life based on what-ifs. It had almost been a relief to hear that she was leaving Boston, enough that he had let his resolve slip and had kissed her again, knowing the temptation she represented would soon be gone forever.

He knocked at Chloe's door and waited. He had promised Chloe that he would help her study for her upcoming board exams and had agreed to come to her while she was still recovering. At first that had been at Tate's and after she had moved home last week they had decided it was easier to keep meeting at her home.

"Hi," she greeted him, as she led him into the living room.

"How are you feeling?" he asked, as he watched her make her way slowly across the room and ease herself back onto the couch. It was hard to dismiss the clinician in him and just be Chloe's friend.

"I have good days and bad days, but Erin says that is normal."

Erin. He had almost convinced himself that he was here just to help Chloe but the moment she spoke Erin's name he knew he had deeper motives. "Have you already seen Erin in follow-up?"

"Yes, last week, and she calls at least once a day to check in on me. Can I get you something to drink?"

"Water, please." He should change the subject. He had already resigned himself to the fact that Erin was not suitable in his life and he should have nothing more to do with her.

"I didn't realize you two were close friends." Damn, guilt washed over him as he realized he was using Chloe to get information on Erin, but he couldn't resist. Erin was still an enigma to him and he needed to know more. Maybe then he would be able to reconcile the past and move on with his life.

"Erin is a pretty private person. I would be, too, if I had gone through everything she has."

"You mean her marriage to Kevin Dufour?"

"I'm not sure I would call that a marriage."

"What do you mean?"

"I mean Kevin Dufour never for one day acted like he was married. I moved to Boston after they were married and the fact that he had a wife never once kept him from making advances on me or any other woman who walked by him."

Ryan inhaled and exhaled slowly as he processed Chloe's words. Did the fact that Kevin was a serial philanderer change things? Certainly it questioned the theory that he had been lured away from a happily committed relationship, as Sabrina had suggested. "Did Erin know?"

Chloe stopped, her facial expression changing, and all of sudden he felt as if he was the one being evaluated. What had started as casual conversation between friends had definitely changed. She paused before she finally answered him. "Eventually, but she didn't see it for a long time. I was with her the day she found a note in her locker anonymously telling her of her husband's affair with the hospital pharmacist."

He winced, both at Chloe's words and at once again wishing he could take back the words he had spoken in anger in Scotland. *You got what you deserved.* If he'd known then what he knew now he never would have spoken them. He murmured under his breath to himself, *"Callous bastard..."* That was how he had behaved.

"There are a lot more words I would use to describe Kevin Dufour, but I don't waste my time and neither does Erin. I'm friends with her because I admire her, Ryan. She walked away from her marriage with her head held high and is an incredible mother to Jennie."

Water lodged in his windpipe and he coughed violently in response. Erin? A mother? Had he heard

Chloe correctly? Confusion coursed through him and he felt as if his chest was being crushed with a vise.

"Erin's a mother?"

"Yes, she has a one-year-old daughter named Jennie. She's beautiful."

One. Erin's daughter was one. His mind flashed back to their night together and the broken condom and Erin's confession. He would have sworn on his life that her infertility had been the thing she hadn't deceived him about. "Did she adopt?"

If he hadn't gotten Chloe's attention before he definitely had it now and he had shown his hand, revealing his knowledge of her infertility. "I didn't realize you knew Erin."

"I know of her from her marriage to Kevin." As much as he didn't like lying to Chloe, he also knew that if Erin hadn't told Chloe about the two of them she would not appreciate Ryan being the one to do so.

"But you knew about her infertility?" Chloe asked skeptically.

"Yes." He wasn't prepared to fabricate a story so instead he acknowledged the truth.

Chloe was silent for a long time before she finally began speaking. "No, she got pregnant around the same time as her divorce became final. Not surprisingly, Kevin has taken no responsibility for the baby, so Erin is a single mother and she's wonderful at it. Jennie is the happiest, most loved baby I have ever seen."

Ryan felt his mind and heart race. Kevin had taken no responsibility for the baby. Was there a reason for that beyond his obvious selfish character flaws? He needed to know more, and he needed to know more now. He looked up at Chloe and knew that she had no more answers for him. There was also no way he was going to be able to sit and focus on helping her study for the next hour. He needed answers now and to get them he needed to talk to Erin.

"Chloe, I just realized there is something I need to tie up back at the hospital urgently. Can I give you a rain check on today and we can try again later on in the week?"

"Sure," she answered, still looking puzzled but not questioning him further.

"Don't worry about getting up. I'll let myself out." He walked back to the large door and looked back at Chloe once more, wondering if she had just been the one to tell him he had a daughter.

Erin led afternoon rounds, her team of junior residents and medical students gathered in the ward's conference room giving verbal updates on the patients.

"How is Mrs. Campbell?" she asked one of the medical students who had just returned from seeing the patient. It was routine to allow the junior residents and medical students independent learning with the patients but she always laid her eyes on every single patient before leaving for the day.

"She's doing better. She was able to walk around the ward this afternoon and tolerated the introduction of food this afternoon."

"Great. Mrs. Gregg?"

"She'll be ready and wanting to be discharged by tomorrow morning," her junior resident responded.

The door to the conference room swung open and the discussion stopped as Ryan entered, walking directly toward her. He wasn't in scrubs but was dressed in a taupe fitted T-shirt and designer denim. He obviously wasn't working.

"I need to talk to you." She wasn't sure if it was clear to the others in the room but it was clear to her that this need did not stem from anything regarding a patient. She looked at her team and tried to figure out how to handle this, instantly worried about what Ryan wanted and his obvious sense of urgency.

"We're just finishing afternoon rounds. I can talk to you in about thirty minutes."

He didn't take her up on her offer. Instead he leaned closer, his voice quieter but no less insistent. "It needs to be now, and I think we should probably talk alone."

She looked out again at their audience, knowing she was powerless to stop this conversation from happening. The least she could do was have it privately.

"Ruth, please finish afternoon rounds while I speak with Dr. Callum. If you have any concerns, please let the on-call resident for the evening know."

She walked from the room, aware that Ryan was following her. She heard him inhale, about to begin their conversation, but she stopped him. "Not here."

She walked farther down the hall until she reached an empty patient room, waiting for him to enter and then closing the door behind her. When she turned back to look at him she knew he knew.

"Tell me about Jennie."

Blood rushed to her ears and she could hear each part of her heart beat as if in slow motion, though she knew it was racing. It didn't even matter how he knew—he knew and all her plans and her life changed now.

"Jennie is my daughter."

"I think you know there is a lot more that I am asking."

She wiped her palms against fitted black slacks before looking up at him. She knew he wasn't going to let this go. She had to make a decision now. How she handled things from here would make all the difference.

"Do you want a paternity test?" It wasn't what he had been expecting. But it was the only way she could buy some time until he found out the truth.

Ryan went from standing to sitting on the empty bed, his hand running through his hair. "So there is the possibility she's mine?"

"Yes." More than a possibility, she couldn't be anyone else's.

"And you didn't tell me?"

"You'd already told me you can't be with a woman like me."

"That has no bearing on whether or not you have been lying and keeping my daughter from me, Erin."

She knew he was angry and didn't want to antagonize him. After she had condemned him in Scotland for lying by omission, she had no ground to stand on.

"Jennie and I are a package deal, Ryan." He needed to know that. That she would never be separated from her daughter.

"You're not going to California."

"What?" She was shocked by the abrupt change in focus.

"You heard me. If Jennie is my daughter you are not taking her across the country away from me."

She wasn't surprised. Hadn't she known that if

Ryan knew about Jennie he would want to be involved? Wasn't that one of the reasons she hadn't told him in the first place? She thought of her fellowship and how long and hard she had worked to earn it. She was amazed that she wasn't going to fight him; Jennie was the most important thing in the world to her and her career was a distant second. From this minute on she needed to do everything possible to prove to Ryan that she wasn't the immoral other woman he believed her to be. She needed him to see who she really was then maybe he wouldn't try to take Jennie away.

"Okay."

She could tell he was ready to argue with her and was not expecting her acquiescence.

"I want to meet her."

"Now?" she asked. "Do you want to wait for the test results instead?"

"No. If she is mine, I don't want to waste another minute apart."

This time she nodded her agreement. She knew she couldn't object because she knew the test results were going to reveal just that. From this moment on everything hinged on him seeing her for the person she was. Maybe even seeing her with Jennie would make him think twice about possible custody demands.

"I need to check on a few of my patients and then we can go."

"I'll wait for you."

She did her afternoon rounds in a daze, hoping that her team had done a good job because she felt as if today she could miss something. Would Ryan see what she saw when she looked at Jennie? His own smaller, feminine reflection looking back at him? It was a chance she was going to have to take.

She finished up in twenty minutes and met him outside the ward's doors. They walked in silence down the hospital corridor toward the parking garage. "You'll need my address. I live at 90 Winchester Avenue."

"I'll follow you there."

Boston traffic was typically heavy, but she wasn't surprised when he didn't lose her tail on the way home. She motioned toward visitors' parking and waited for him at her building's elevator.

"You live in an apartment?"

She found herself bristling at his question but reminded herself she needed to keep her cool. "Yes, I decided that it was better to live closer to the hospital so that I could spend more time with Jennie rather than commuting. The building has a lovely children's play park that Jennie goes to daily."

"Who watches her while you're working?"

"Her nanny, Carolyn. She's been with us since Jennie was three months old and is wonderful with her."

He didn't ask her any more questions as they rode up in the elevator together. She walked to the end of the hallway and unlocked the door to her three-bedroom apartment. From the entry she walked to the combined open dining, kitchen and living room. She saw Jennie playing with her wooden puzzle on her play mat in the living room and, as always, the best part of her day was watching her daughter's face light up when she saw her. "Mum, mum, mum, mum," Jennie repeated, as she pushed herself onto her pudgy legs and with her usual unsteady walk made her way to Erin. Her arms extended upward the moment she ran into Erin's legs.

"Hello, my sweetheart." She brushed her daughter's brown hair back and kissed her cheek.

Carolyn emerged from the kitchen, pausing only slightly at the sight of Ryan. Erin had never before brought a man home and she was impressed that Carolyn was handling the surprise so well.

"How was she today?" Erin asked.

"Great. She had her normal naps and we spent most of the afternoon at the park. Supper is ready in the kitchen for you both. I'll see you in the morning."

"Thanks, Carolyn."

The other woman let herself out and Erin turned back to Ryan, but his attention was entirely on Jennie, who seemed equally transfixed by the new person in her life. Watching them together made Erin's heart cry and question every decision she had made since the moment she'd found out she was pregnant.

She shifted Jennie onto her hip. "This is mummy's friend Ryan."

His eyes broke from Jennie's and he looked up at her. She couldn't introduce him as her father, not yet. "Do you want to show Ryan your puzzle?"

She watched as Jennie evaluated Ryan and then nodded in agreement. She walked with Jennie over to the play mat, sitting them both on the floor and waiting for Ryan to do the same. He did, but he still seemed overwhelmed so Erin took the lead. "Show Ryan where the sun goes." And she handed Jennie the piece.

It was Jennie's favorite puzzle and she took no time

to place the piece near its slot and then with the awkwardness of a toddler wiggled it in. She looked up at Ryan expectantly.

"You're a smart girl. Do you want to show me where the balloon goes?" He handed her the red, round puzzle piece. She reached out her little hand and took it from him, placing it in the same fashion as the previous piece and then looking back at him. "Good job."

Erin stayed silent as the two worked together to complete the rest of the puzzle. When they were finished two pairs of identical eyes looked up at her. "Would you like to stay for dinner?"

"Yes."

She lifted Jennie from the floor and carried her toward the eat-in kitchen, securing her in the high chair. Carolyn had prepared a large Cobb salad and Erin picked out small pieces for Jennie, putting them on her tray, and also served two plates for her and Ryan. She opened the fridge, holding up a bottle of wine, and Ryan nodded agreement and she poured two glasses, as well.

The meal was a typical one for Erin. Erin ate while at the same time watching Jennie get as much food on the floor and high chair as she did into her mouth. After dinner Ryan made no attempt to leave so she included him in their bathtime and bedtime rituals. "Good night, my love," she murmured sweetly, before gently covering her daughter. She closed the door and returned to the living room, where Ryan was seated on the couch.

She went to the fridge and refilled their glasses of wine before joining him.

"I don't know what to say to you. She's a happy,

healthy, wonderful little girl and part of me is grateful and the other part of me will never forgive you for keeping her from me if she's mine."

It was honest and it was fair and she couldn't argue against his feelings. "I'm sorry."

"Why? How could you do something like this?"

She wished he would yell at her. Yelling would be better than hearing the pain come through his confused, calm voice.

"Do you know what Jennie means?" It wasn't the immediate answer to his question but the best explanation she had. "It means 'God is gracious' and ever since I found out I was pregnant that has been my only thought. Jennie is my miracle, the baby I desperately wanted and never thought I would have. Since the moment I found out I was pregnant I have been terrified of losing her."

"You thought I would take her away?"

"The last time I saw you you made it clear that I was the last woman in the world you would want to be the mother of your child."

"And that gave you the right to possibly keep me from my child?"

She did her best not to rise to his accusations. "It took away any sense of trust I had in you."

"So now we're even, except this time the consequences are considerably higher. Can you organize the paternity test?"

"Yes."

"I want answers, Erin."

Ryan stood in the hospital's large garden, waiting. It was the last day in June and the annual graduation ceremony for the finishing residents. The sun was hot but a breeze off the water dampened its effects.

As a member of the staff who was closely involved in resident education he had been asked to speak at the commencement, but his mind was distracted from his requested purpose. He looked through the crowd, waiting for Erin to arrive. Finally he spotted them. Erin was walking through the crowd, beautiful in a sleeveless midlength turquoise lace dress that was tied with a simple black ribbon belt. In her arms she held Jennie, who was wearing a vibrant red summer dress and was happily looking around the crowd. He had never seen Erin look more beautiful.

At his request Erin had sent him a photo of Jennie and since then he hadn't been able to keep his eyes off it. It would take time to do the paternity test and get the results back, and until then all he had were his gut instincts. Those instincts were telling him Jennie was his child. Her hair was darker than Erin's, more like his. She had Erin's nose and mouth but her eyes reminded him of his. Her smile was definitely her own. He couldn't imagine that a child so wonderful could ever be a part of Kevin Dufour.

When he wasn't thinking of Jennie he was thinking of Erin. He had heard her explanation and her apology, but that didn't change the anger he felt over missing the first one and a half years of his probable daughter's life. He still felt as if he didn't know her. He had thought he had known her in Edinburgh, but her past with Kevin had changed his mind. Now he had competing thoughts of her inside his head.

There was his first impression of the honest, caring woman he had taken to bed. Then she had been portrayed as the other woman, the image his sister had supplied. He had worked with her enough in the past few weeks to know she was a competent, dedicated physician, and he respected her for it. And now he knew her as a mother, which brought with it the double-edged sword of watching how wonderful she was with Jennie and knowing that she had deliberately kept her from him.

He walked up to the both of them. "Congratulations."

"Thank you."

"What are your plans now that you are no longer a resident?" He thought it was a casual question but he could tell that he had set her on edge.

"I did as you asked and declined the fellowship in California. Very graciously Boston General has offered me a temporary position pending a formal hiring process."

He hadn't considered the ramifications to her career when he had insisted she not move to California. But it spoke volumes about her that the hospital had been willing to offer her a position on short notice. He hadn't been wrong about the type of physician he knew her to be.

She looked around before she resumed talking. "I talked to the laboratory and arranged the testing. You can go and give a blood sample at any time. All Jennie needs is a cheek swab that I'll do as soon as I can and then we should have the results in a few weeks."

He looked between the two, Jennie happy and content on her mother's hip, and knew what he needed to do. The two were a pair and he would never separate them for either of their sakes.

"I think we need to start again."

"I don't understand what you mean." Neither did he. What was it that he wanted from Erin?

"There was a time when both of us were very compatible and very much in sync. I think the best thing for Jennie would be if we tried to get back to a time where we trusted each other."

"I don't know if that's possible."

"It was once. Maybe it will be again if we actually take the time to get to know each other and put aside our joint pasts."

Erin wasn't prepared for Ryan's suggestion, but she couldn't fault his reasoning. There had been a time when she had trusted him, she just didn't know if it would be possible to get that back. Regardless, being given a chance to prove to him that she was a good mother before he learned for sure Jennie was his was an opportunity she wasn't going to let slip away.

"Okay, I think you're right but I have no idea where to even begin."

"What are you doing after this?"

"Jennie and I are going to the Hamptons. My parents have a house on the beach and now that I am done with residency I thought it would be the perfect time to take Jennie for a weekend away before I start my new position next week."

"I'll come with you."

"I don't know." She was hesitant. Was she ready to be alone with Ryan for that period of time? So far all their interactions in Boston had been centered around work or Jennie. The one and only time they had been alone together he had kissed her and even though it had been just once, every inch of her body remembered what she wanted from him. What would happen between them each night after Jennie went to bed?

"I do. We need this time together. When the results come back we need to have something to build on together."

He was more right than he knew so she couldn't disagree. "We are already packed and ready to go. If you don't mind driving with us, we can pick you up after the ceremony."

"Agreed." He looked down at the program he was holding. "You're speaking, as well?"

Erin smiled "Chloe and Kate nominated me to represent the chiefs. It's an honor."

"Then we'll pick up where we left off in Scotland. Hopefully this will go better than the last time we spoke in public together."

CHAPTER ELEVEN

ERIN PULLED UP to Ryan's brownstone townhouse and immediately became envious. The old brick facade and heritage trees that surrounded the yard were warm and inviting. She looked back at Jennie, who was playing happily in her car seat. This was going to be one of her homes and Erin felt emptiness at the possibility of Jennie and Ryan here together without her.

She saw Ryan lock the front door and head toward her with a small bag. He had changed into gray linen shorts and a teal-colored polo shirt. She could see glimpses of both tattoos and she knew without having to take a breath that he would smell of sweat and sunshine, just as he had the day they'd met. She wrapped her hair in her hands and lifted it from her neck to cool the heat from her body. She was happy she had changed into shorts and a loose-fitting thin cotton T-shirt.

She got out and met him at the hatch of her crossover. "Do you want to drive?"

"Sure." He took the keys from her outstretched hand. The brush of his fingers against hers was both surprisingly familiar and arousing. What had she gotten herself into?

The trip to the Hamptons was long, but not as arduous as she had worried it might have turned out to be. Jennie stayed content and they stopped frequently to let her move around and snack. She fell asleep and slept the last few hours as evening progressed into night. She and Ryan stuck to safe topics. Now that they had their careers in common there was a lot of shared experience to draw on for conversation. At times she even found herself forgetting that there should be awkwardness between them.

It was dark, the sky lit only by the stars as she directed them to her parents' beachfront house. "It's not large," she cautioned him. "My stepfather is a doctor, not the CEO of an international company."

Ryan laughed. "I know who your stepfather is, Erin. I believe he is my boss."

"True." And Erin joined his laughter.

As Ryan shut off the engine they both looked back at Jennie. Her head was tilted all the way to her shoulder and her eyes were shut, body relaxed. "I'll get her if you want to get the door," Erin suggested.

She unfastened the child belts and enjoyed the moment when the little girl relaxed back into her arms. Ryan held open the door for her and she went into the house, leaving it dark so as not to wake her. Ryan seemed to understand and he wordlessly emptied the back of her vehicle and brought in all their belongings.

The house had two bedrooms, a single bathroom and a combined living room and kitchen. Its interior was classic cape-side, with white wainscoting and wooden floors. It was furnished with comfortable light-colored furniture and accents of bright yellows and oranges. The best feature was the patio that looked out onto the beach and ocean. Most of Erin's happiest childhood memories had been made at the beach house and she had dreamed of the day when she could bring her own children here to share it.

"Where do you want her crib?" he asked. She had planned to take the master bedroom and set Jennie's portable crib in the other bedroom but she quickly realized that wasn't going to work with Ryan. His tall frame would never comfortably fit into one of the two single beds in the guest room.

"The room at the end of the hall on the left, please."

She waited until he reappeared in the hall before bringing Jennie to bed. She wasn't surprised that Ryan had had no problem assembling the complicated device and had found the sheets she had packed. She smiled at the turned-down blankets.

"I love you, my sweetheart," she murmured, as she kissed Jennie's cheek and laid her in the crib.

With a final look she left her to sleep. "She's beautiful when she sleeps," Ryan commented, still not making any move to leave the small bedroom.

Guilt swept her again. Should she tell him now that he was Jennie's father? For the first time since Scotland they'd had several hours together that had been not only pleasant but enjoyable, with no confrontations or accusations. What would happen if she told him now? Would he even believe her?

"Yes, she is," she answered simply.

He joined her in the kitchen. "Can I get you something? I had the caretaker stock the fridge for the weekend."

"I'll have whatever you're having."

She opened the fridge and discovered a bottle of

champagne tied with a red ribbon and small envelope attached. She took out the bottle and opened the card.

Congratulations, Erin.
We couldn't be more proud of you.
Mom & Stephen.

She showed Ryan the card as a means of explanation. She didn't want him to think her plans had been to drink alone in the beach house for the weekend with a small child. "We should open it," he recommended.

She handed him the bottle and got out two wine glasses. Ryan opened the bottle, the pop and emerging foam reminding her that this was indeed an occasion to be celebrated.

"I should show you the patio. It's the best part of the house." She led the way through the French doors and took her place on one of the covered wicker patio chairs, drawing her legs under her. Ryan joined her, sitting across from her, in the still of the night.

"Congratulations, Erin. I know it hasn't been the easiest journey for you and you should be proud of your accomplishment."

She was stunned by the generosity of his comments. He could easily have argued that it didn't have to be as hard as she had made it if she had only made better choices, particularly asking for his help with their daughter. Instead he didn't and she felt proud of herself, as well.

"Thank you."

"You seem to be getting along better with your parents. The last time we talked you thought they were disappointed in you."

"It's amazing what having a child does to your point of view. I realized when I had Jennie that I could never be disappointed in her, just her choices. And looking back, I made some choices that were worthy of their disappointment."

"So being a single mother didn't add to their disappointment?"

"No, I was worried when I told them, but both Mom and Stephen were wonderful. I think, like me, they had lost hope of ever having a grandchild and they see Jennie as the wonderful miracle she is."

"You call your stepfather Stephen?"

"Yes. My mother remarried when I was fourteen. She was ready and I wasn't. I loved my dad—he was my hero—and there was only ever one of him."

Through the darkness she could see Ryan's face and knew what he was thinking. They were the same thoughts she was having now. How could she deprive Jennie of a father when losing hers had been so hard for her?

She took another sip from her glass and let the cool, dry bubbles pass down her throat. "I wasn't thinking clearly, Ryan. Maybe I'm still not. When I found out I was pregnant all I could think about was not losing her."

"I know, Erin. You've apologized already and you don't need to keep doing it. I need to accept my responsibility in this situation, too."

He walked over to the patio rail and faced the ocean with his back to her. She remembered what it was like to direct most of the anger inward. It was the same way she'd felt when she'd finally left Kevin. She knew she had to give him space, but also remembered how much that anger had turned to an aching pain. So she simply stood and joined him at the rail.

"One of my favorite things about the world is the sky, no matter where you are," Ryan shared.

She stared up with him, enjoying the pitch-blackness she never saw in Boston. "That must have been comforting when you were in the military. Do you miss it?"

"At times. But it was also time to move on with my life."

"Would you have come to Boston General if you'd known I was there?" She moved her eyes from the sky to the man standing above her.

"Honestly, no, I wouldn't have."

"I offended you that badly?" Now it was her turn to be hurt.

"No, you confused me. I didn't understand how the woman I had met equated with what I had learned about your past."

"And that was enough to keep you away?"

He brushed her hair from her face, his hand resting on her cheek. "No, I stayed away because, despite everything, I was still attracted to you. I still am."

She realized she had lifted herself and was straining toward him only a moment before his head came down and his lips touched hers. She could taste the champagne on his lips as they brushed against hers. It was the softest of touches before a gentle pressure opened her to him and he deepened their kiss. If she had been capable of rational thought she would have wondered how this man, despite everything, could still cause her to feel such passion, but she couldn't think, not even when he broke away.

"This wasn't my plan." He shook his head slightly.

"I…I…" Still she didn't know what to think or say.

"When I said we should get back to the place we had been in Scotland, I didn't mean physically."

"Oh." And she was embarrassed by just how much disappointment she felt. She, too, had absolutely no plans for anything romantic or physical between them, deeming that dream well lost, but the reminder of what they had once experienced together was enough to make her feel bereft again as he pulled away.

"You should go to bed."

"Your room is the one down the other hall. I'll see you in the morning."

Erin walked quietly to the room she was sharing with Jennie, taking a moment to cover her daughter, who always managed to kick off her blankets. She looked at Jennie, the sight of their daughter giving her the strong reminder she needed—that this was not just about her and Ryan. The option for a fleeting love affair had ended in Scotland. She couldn't do anything that would jeopardize their relationship because, despite her attraction and growing romantic feelings toward him, he was Jennie's father first and foremost. Now Jennie had a father, and Erin remembered how she had treasured hers for the short time he had been in her life, Erin wasn't going to be responsible for taking that away from her daughter.

Erin awoke to the sun streaming in through the windows and the smell of the ocean in the air. She glanced at the clock and blinked. When had been the last time she had slept past eight? She immediately glanced at the crib, only to find it empty. Panic sparked inside her as she scrambled to find Jennie.

She didn't have to look far. Jennie was sitting in the center of the living room floor amid the toys Erin had packed for her, Ryan by her side. She exhaled, not even considering concealing the fear she had been feeling.

Ryan looked up at her and realized her alarm. "I'm sorry, I heard her playing in her crib and thought I would get her so that you could sleep. I didn't mean to scare you."

She was afraid and upset, but one look at Jennie and she knew she couldn't share any of those feelings. The little girl was beaming with happiness and she didn't want to upset her.

"It's okay. I guess I'm just not used to having help." She wanted to take back the words the minute she'd said them, realizing that the reason she didn't have help had been her own choice. She looked at Ryan and respected him even more for letting her comment pass.

"What are your plans for the day?" he asked.

"Not much," she confessed. "I really thought we would just go down to the beach and play in the sand and then maybe check out the farmers' market this afternoon."

"Sounds great."

She walked to the kitchen to make a cup of coffee and noticed the pot was already brewed.

"I remembered," Ryan commented, from the living room.

She poured herself a cup and took a sip of the hot, dark, full-bodied roast. It wasn't until that moment that she realized what she was wearing. In her haste to find Jennie she hadn't had time to pull on her robe so instead she was standing in the kitchen in nothing but an oversize T-shirt, her legs bare. She looked up and saw Ryan watching her and she self-consciously slipped behind the kitchen island. The kiss from last night was still very much on her mind.

He smiled at her not-so-subtle move and she heard the faint laugh coming from his lips.

"It's okay. It's nothing I haven't seen before."

She blushed and then blushed harder, remembering in just what state he had seen her.

"On your balcony in Scotland. The first night we met you weren't very shy about your choice in pajamas then, either." His explanation should have been comforting, except that she realized he had offered it because of the alternative he had guessed she was recollecting.

"If you are okay with her, I'll go get dressed."

"We're fine. Take your time."

She showered and dressed quickly, not used to having the extra time. She had packed before she'd known Ryan was coming and looked down at the meager options before her. She didn't spend too much time thinking about what was making her want to look her best. In the end she didn't have much choice, so she settled on what she had planned she would wear when she had thought it was just going to be her and Jennie, her emerald-green bikini with its matching cover-up. She blew her hair dry and then looked in the mirror, forgoing any makeup in favor of sunscreen alone.

Jennie and Ryan were still playing when she finished. She picked out Jennie's protective sun shirt and shorts and dressed her, being careful to apply sunblock to all her exposed skin.

"Ready?" Ryan asked.

"Yes."

It was nice having the extra hands as they made their way down to the beach. Between beach chairs, a blanket, toys, snacks and Jennie herself, Erin would have had her hands full. They picked a spot on the sand and immediately Jennie dumped a bucket of sand in the center of the blanket.

"Nice." Ryan laughed before picking up the little girl and swinging her round. Her shrieks of delight filled the air.

The three of them played for the next two hours and Erin couldn't remember when she had been this relaxed or seen Jennie as happy. The look on her face when Ryan dipped her feet into the ocean for the first time was amazing. They ate a picnic lunch and then headed to the market.

A different time, a different place, but as the day went on Erin realized that Ryan had been right. This was what they needed. A chance, away from everyone else and their past, to get to know each other again. She also realized what she had been missing. What it would be like to raise Jennie with two parents, a partner for all the joys and challenges that lay ahead.

They made a light salad for supper and participated in the nightly bath ritual together. "It's a wonder there's any sand still on the beach!" Ryan commented, as the water drained and the entire bottom of the tub was full of sand.

Erin laughed but her attention was on Jennie. It had been a great day, a busy day, and Jennie had barely napped and showed no signs of willingness to sleep any time soon. She had a bad feeling about where this was headed. Sure enough, the simple act of putting her in her pajamas was the last straw and Jennie began to cry. The cry progressed to earsplitting wails as Erin struggled in vain to soothe her.

It was impossible as the little girl rubbed her head back and forth into Erin's neck and shoulder, large, wet tears streaming down her face.

"What's wrong with her?" Ryan asked, Jennie's complete meltdown a new experience for him, as well.

"She's overtired," Erin answered very quietly, begging Jennie to stop.

The more Jennie cried the more distressed they both became. Erin walked up and down the short hallway, whispering reassurances to her daughter, but nothing worked. It wasn't Jennie's first meltdown and normally Erin would have been more relaxed and let it run its course, but not in front of Ryan. She needed to prove she was a good mother and what kind of mother couldn't soothe her little girl?

More tears, only this time Erin's as Jennie's wailing continued. She put her down, but she only cried harder, her arms reaching up for her mother.

"Here, let me take her." Ryan's words broke through the cries.

She wanted to say no, that she could do it, but she couldn't and she wasn't in a state to argue that she had control of the situation. She passed Jennie to him and her wails increased for a minute before there was silence, a few more cries, and more silence. Erin wiped away her own tears and saw Ryan gently rubbing Jennie's back, her little face pressed against his chest as he walked the halls with her.

A few minutes later she was out cold, her body limp in Ryan's arms. Erin walked with him to their bedroom, watching as he laid her in the crib and covered her. "Good night, my sweetheart." She bent down to kiss the still-wet cheek softly.

They carefully closed the door and retreated, the house now eerily quiet in the aftermath of the meltdown. She took a seat on the couch, moving one of the orange pillows to hold it protectively in front of her.

"I'm sorry," she said, her nerves totally shot both from Jennie's crying and her inability to soothe her in front of Ryan. What must he be thinking of her mothering skills?

"Why are you sorry?" He sat beside her on the couch.

"I couldn't comfort her."

"That's okay."

"No, it's not. I'm her mother, I'm supposed to be able to comfort her."

"Erin—" he started, but she interrupted him.

"I don't want you to think I'm a bad mother." She moved her hand to her mouth the moment the words escaped. It was another example of her inability to keep her thoughts to herself in front of him.

"No one is perfect all the time, not you, not Jennie."

"I'm so afraid you are going to take her away from me." Now that she had started there was no stopping her and her own tears resurfaced.

He reached forward, taking away the pillow she held between them, turning his whole body toward her. He looked more confused than ever. "Why would I take her away?"

"Because you don't think I'm a good person, because maybe you won't think I'm a good enough mother. I wanted this weekend to go well, to prove to you I was a good mother to our daughter."

"That's the first time you've ever called her our daughter." Ryan's voice was soft.

She had, and there was no going back. Just spending the day with Ryan as a family, she'd realized that Jennie wasn't just hers, she was theirs, together. She also no longer just wanted Jennie as her family, she wanted it to include Ryan.

"She has your eyes."

"I know," he admitted.

She looked at him, feeling more vulnerable than she had when they'd first met on that hillside in Scotland. "What are we going to do?"

"What do you want?"

"I want to do what's best for Jennie."

"And what about you?"

"I'm not important."

"To me you are."

His words could not have been more perfect. As her feelings for Ryan had resurfaced one of her fears had been that she would be the consolation prize that came with his daughter. She needed him to tell her otherwise, to prove to her otherwise.

"Kiss me," she said quietly.

"I can't." She looked up at him and she started to pull away but he grabbed both her hands, keeping her facing him.

"I can't just kiss you. I want you too badly just to kiss you."

She understood everything he was saying so instead she leaned in and kissed him. Everything about the taste of his lips, the feel of his skin and the smell of him was familiar, so much so that it instantaneously sparked a fire inside her. The first time they had been together she'd thought she had wanted him, but she had been wrong then, because nothing compared to the desperate need she felt now.

He broke away and lifted her from the couch and into his arms. She didn't ask where they were headed as Ryan carried her to the master bedroom. He pulled off his shirt before coming down on her on the bed, his lips finding hers and his tongue exploring and tasting her. She wove her hands into his short hair, holding him to her. She never wanted the kiss to end but at the same time she wanted more.

She felt him rise slightly from her, his arm a study in flexed muscular perfection. The casual beach shorts and jersey halter top she had changed into after the beach gave him no bother as he quickly stripped her naked and then did the same with his own clothes. The bedroom window was open and she could smell and feel the night's ocean air against her skin. Between the slight coolness of the air and her anticipation she felt as if her whole body was trembling in want of him, every hair in every pore poised for his next move.

He didn't leave her waiting for long and soon there was nothing cool about the feel of his completely naked hard muscular body hotly pressed against her. He paused, looking into her eyes, and she felt she could drown in the depths of the blue. He wanted her, too. She arched her back, pressing herself even more against him, feeling every inch of him and his want for her.

His hand swept up her side and over her tattoo before his hand cupped her breast, his thumb stroking her nipple. She didn't have to wait long before he caressed the swollen tip with his mouth.

The more he touched her the more she wanted him and she could feel her body readying for him as she unconsciously spread herself more and more open for him.

"You're even more beautiful than I remembered," he murmured, his breath hot against her breast.

"I need you." And truer words were never spoken. She needed him to make love to her, she needed him to be a father to their daughter and she needed him to love her because she knew she was in love with him.

He broke away from her, reaching into his shaving kit to bring out a small foil wrapper. She didn't miss the look of irony on his face as he sheathed himself. He kneeled between her legs, his hand stroking upward from her ankle to the top of her thigh. Without thinking, she wrapped both legs around him moments before he pushed into her.

It had been over two years since she'd had this feeling. The last time she had been touched so intimately had been with Ryan and she had never wanted any other man. She found herself matching his every movement. Their rocking back and forth echoed the waves of the ocean heard through the open window. As she reached ever nearer to her climax she wanted even more from him and she moved her hands from their strong hold on his back to touch his hands. He immediately took hold, lacing his fingers through hers. Now with each movement she felt truly complete. As Ryan pushed deeper each movement moved her closer to the edge, his virile length hitting hard against her core, her breasts pressed hard against his chest, her hands in his being pressed into the mattress as each mini-peak was met with the sound of the waves crashing on the beach.

Then she could hold on no longer. She moved both her legs behind his back, locking her ankles, and with one final stroke she pushed herself hard against him as his mouth came down on hers, stifling both their cries of ecstasy.

They stayed like that for a long time before he finally pulled away from her, only briefly to discard the condom, before he pulled her against him and the sheet over both of them, their sweat-covered bodies cooling quickly in the night air.

"I think that is the only thing that hasn't changed between us," Ryan murmured against the back of her neck.

"Mmm…" she moaned, still in a satiated fog.

"The last time we were together was the most passionate night I had ever had, until now."

He had more of her attention now, as she thought back to the revelation she'd had right before they'd made love. She loved Ryan. She was in love with Ryan and she desperately needed him to love her, too. She waited, but her hopes of hearing those words were dashed as she recognized the gentle repetition of his breath signaling he was asleep.

* * *

The next few days were almost perfect. They spent their days as a family, going to the beach, exploring the public gardens, and after Jennie went to bed their nights exploring each other. Neither Ryan nor Erin did anything to ruin the budding relationship between them. They never spoke of their past, his sister, and Ryan didn't ask her any more questions about Jennie's possible paternity.

They celebrated the Fourth of July sitting together on the beachfront patio, watching the fireworks with Jennie, who barely managed to keep her eyes open in Ryan's arms.

The next day it was time to return to reality and Erin felt uneasiness build. They had been perfect together in Scotland. Perfect together again here in the Hamptons as a family. But what would happen when they had to face the realities of their lives together in Boston? What would happen when the paternity test definitively proved Ryan to be Jennie's father? Would he want to be a family? Could she continue in their relationship just waiting and hoping he fell in love with her?

Eventually they would also have to face their past. She knew he loved his sister and she had no idea how Sabrina would take the news of Erin's involvement in her brother's life. She had wanted to explain to him the truth about her past with Sabrina and Kevin, but was afraid to ruin the ideal of their family time together by bringing up such an unsavory subject. Was their relationship strong enough to overcome his family's disapproval, and what would happen if it wasn't?

CHAPTER TWELVE

THREE WEEKS AFTER their return Ryan felt sure about what he needed to do. Without discussion he had practically been living with Erin and Jennie and he had never been happier with his life. Every day he felt even closer to Erin and Jennie. He had done the bloodwork more to confirm paternity. He wanted the world to know that Jennie was his daughter.

The heat from the late July afternoon hit him as he opened his car door and walked along the stone path toward Sabrina's front door. Her house was a suburban family home in Cambridge only a few blocks from their parents' and perfect for her growing family. The neighborhood was filled with children running and playing outside and he thought about how much he wanted that for Jennie.

Ryan rang the doorbell and waited for an answer.

Sabrina answered the door and the similarity between Sabrina and Jennie struck him instantly. All of his features he saw in Jennie he also saw in Sabrina. She was dressed casually in capri pants, a loose-fitting T-shirt and with a beaded necklace his nephew, Simon, was struggling to grab and put in his mouth. "Well, this is a surprise!" Sabrina exclaimed, as she reached out and gave him a one-armed hug. "What's the occasion?"

"Can't I just stop by and see my little sister and nephew?" he asked her casually, knowing there was much more behind his visit, and that Sabrina knew that, too.

"You can, but you don't," she teased.

She was right so he didn't disagree. "Can I come in?"

"Of course." She walked with him to the heart of her home, the kitchen, and he took a seat at one of the barstools that lined her granite-covered island. "So are you going to tell me what is wrong?"

"How do you know something is wrong?"

"Because my very important doctor big brother does not just drop by on a weekday in the middle of the afternoon."

"I need to talk to you about something and I'm not sure you are going to like what I have to say."

"Then just say it. I'm not as fragile as you think I am, Ryan."

He was taken aback at her comment and took a moment to truly look at her. She was right. She didn't look fragile. She actually looked nothing like his memory of the depressed, broken woman she had been. Instead, she looked relaxed and at peace and he began to wonder if he had been making decisions to protect her when she didn't need his protection after all.

"I need to talk to you about Erin Dufour." He watched her carefully and she didn't appear anything but surprised.

"That wasn't what I was expecting to hear." She

placed Simon in his baby swing and came around to sit on the barstool opposite him.

"I met her at Boston General. She goes by her maiden name, Madden, now."

"I know," she replied simply.

"You know?" He couldn't hide his shock.

"I met her a few months ago when I had Simon. She didn't recognize me with all the swelling from my pregnancy and my new last name but I recognized her."

"You never said anything." He still couldn't believe what he was hearing.

"You never asked. Why are we talking about Erin?"

"I had a brief relationship with her two years ago before I knew who she was." He looked at his sister carefully, trying to read her response. "When I realized she was Kevin's ex-wife I broke it off."

"Why would you do that?" Sabrina appeared genuinely confused and he felt frustrated at having to explain his motivation.

"Because of what she did to you. The pain she caused you."

"She saved my life. She saved Simon's life."

"What?" This conversation was reaching surreal proportions and his sister's revelations were doing nothing to ease the turmoil inside him.

"When I was pregnant with Simon and started feeling unwell she was the only person who really took me seriously when I said something was wrong. When the others tried to send me home she refused and she ordered the testing that diagnosed my preeclampsia."

"So you forgave her because she took care of you in your pregnancy?"

"There was nothing to forgive."

"What about her affair with Kevin?" He hated having to remind Sabrina of it, hated having to remind himself of Erin's marriage.

"It saved me from a serious mistake. When Kevin first broke off our relationship I was devastated. I wasn't ready to face the fact that the man I loved, whom I had built all my dreams around, had really cheated on me with another woman, so instead I placed all the blame on Erin. It wasn't until after she had married Kevin that I had the courage to confront her. She had no idea who I was, never mind that she had been the other woman. That was when I realized that that man I spent the past four years with had been a liar and a cheat. I felt used, and foolish, and ashamed, and those feelings were the catalyst for my depression."

He wanted to talk more about Erin, but this was the most Sabrina had ever shared with him about her depression and he couldn't dismiss her admission.

"I thought you still blamed Erin. I didn't realize you felt differently. Why didn't you say something back then? I still blame myself for not being there to help you."

"You were away saving the world and I didn't want to bother you with my problems. My feelings didn't seem as important as the wars that you were helping to fight and the lives you were saving."

"I wish you had." For all of their sakes, how he wished he had known.

"Is that why we are talking about Erin?"

"I've been fighting my feelings for her for the past two years, thinking I was betraying you."

"Oh, Ryan." Sabrina was gently shaking her head from side to side.

"She has a daughter, Jennie. She's a year and a half and I'm sure she's mine."

"Oh, my God! When did you find out about her? Why didn't Erin tell you about her?"

"Because before she had Jennie the last time we saw each other I accused her of being an immoral other woman who seduces and traps other women's men." Even to his own ears it sounded horrible and Erin's reaction in not telling him when she had learned of the pregnancy became more clear to him.

"You didn't!"

"Not in those exact words, but the point was made."

"I understand, then," Sabrina commented.

"You agree with her keeping Jennie a secret from me?" Now it was his turn to feel betrayed.

"I understand how on the heels of her divorce from a man who spent their entire relationship violating her trust, she wasn't keen to give you the benefit of the doubt. So what are you going to do?"

"I don't know. I still don't understand why she never told me the truth about her and Kevin."

"Maybe because it's humiliating and embarrassing to admit that you were in love with a man who not only didn't love you but also had no respect for you as a woman?"

He let Sabrina's words sink through him, but she didn't stop there. "Or maybe because it's even worse after going through that to put your trust in a new man, only to find out he thinks the worst of you, too."

"Okay, I get the point." He felt totally unworthy of having Erin in his life.

"So what are you going to do?"

"Tell her I love her and ask her to marry me." Something he regretted not doing sooner. If anything, his conversation with Sabrina had highlighted how lucky he was to still have Erin in his life. Jennie really was a miracle. If it hadn't been for her they wouldn't have found their way back to one another.

"Oh, Ry, you haven't even told her you love her yet?"

"No." He didn't need Sabrina to highlight how foolish he had been.

"Watch Simon. I'll be right back."

He looked over at his nephew and couldn't help but think of everything he had missed with Jennie. Over the past weeks Erin had shared with him her baby albums and videos but it hadn't been the same. Erin hadn't cheated him—he had cheated himself out of Jennie's first year of life.

"Here." She handed him a square velvet box.

"What's this?"

"It's Grandma's engagement ring. Mom gave up hope years ago that you would ever settle down and marry so she gave it to me. I think Erin should have it."

He opened the box to discover the platinum ring that was handcrafted with intricate trellis-like embellishments that led to a central circular diamond that was surrounded by a circle of smaller diamonds. "It's perfect. Are you sure?"

"Yes. I can't think of a woman I would want more as a sister and you need to secure her place in our family as soon as possible. Simon wants to meet his cousin and I want to meet my niece!"

"Thank you, for everything." He stood and hugged his sister, more grateful than she would ever know.

He left Sabrina's finally feeling as if he had the answers. Even after their weekend in the Hamptons he hadn't been able to put together who Erin was completely. He didn't understand how the woman he knew could ever have been the other woman, but now everything made sense. His only regret was not recognizing sooner that Erin could never deliberately hurt anyone. Erin was the same woman he'd fallen for in Scotland, the woman he'd fallen in love with in the Hamptons and the mother of his child. If he was lucky, she would agree to be his wife.

He looked at the ring box and wondered how he was going to make it through the weekend. Erin and Jennie had gone away for her friend Kate's wedding and it would be another four days before he could tell her he loved her.

Long weekends were notorious for the emergency department. Alcohol and an above-average sense of fearlessness typically led to at least a 20 percent increase in volume. Ryan was happy to be busy. His evening shift was taking his mind off waiting for Erin and Jennie to return home.

The emergency medical services dispatch radio sounded. They were ten minutes away with a motor vehicle accident trauma.

"Activate the trauma team," he told the unit clerk, and she keyed in the single code that paged the eight-person team to the trauma bay.

He arrived at the trauma bay and looked around to

make sure all the required equipment was there before donning a protective gown and goggles. Three nurses, a respiratory therapist and one of the emergency medicine residents gathered with him. One of the orthopedic and general surgery residents soon followed.

He could hear the sirens as they approached and could tell the ambulance was racing toward them. It arrived less than a minute later, driving through the bay and coming to an abrupt stop outside the doors. He went through the automatic glass doors and helped the team unload the stretcher, getting a good look at the patient.

He recognized the paramedic, who began to give report. "Restrained middle-aged male involved in a frontal collision. Lost consciousness at the scene and was intubated for airway protection. Obvious open femur fracture."

Ryan glanced down to the man's thigh and saw the protruding bone.

The team moved quickly into the trauma room, and each person specialized in their particular role began their assessment. He gave them three minutes before he intervened. "What do you want to do?" he asked his resident.

"Stabilize, transfuse for blood loss and get full-body imaging to ensure that we are not being distracted by the femur and missing something worse."

"I agree."

He stood in the doorway for the next thirty minutes, being unobtrusive but also making sure the patient was receiving optimal care.

"Why haven't you booked the femur for the operating room?" he heard a voice yell down the hall. It was a voice he had no desire to hear. He looked down the hall to see Kevin Dufour yelling at the trauma team orthopedic resident and now making his way toward them.

"I want this patient in the operating room now," he yelled at the remaining residents and nursing staff. The team paused and looked at Ryan.

"Stick with the plan. Dr. Dufour, can I speak to you for a moment?"

"I want that patient in the operating room now," Kevin seethed.

Ryan did his best to remain calm, which was the opposite of what he really wanted to do. "The patient is still to be stabilized and still needs to have his imaging survey completed to ensure there are no more serious injuries before you spend three hours fixing his femur."

"His femur is his most serious injury, isn't that obvious?"

"No, it's not, which is why we have ordered a CT of his head, chest, abdomen and pelvis."

"I'm in charge here, and I want him transferred to the operating room."

"No, you are not. This man is a patient of the emergency department and under my care and will remain so until I choose otherwise."

"We'll see about that."

Ryan paid no attention to Dufour's exit and returned to his patient.

Twenty minutes later he received verbal report from the radiologist. The victim had an extradural hemorrhage in his brain, requiring immediate evacuation in order to help prevent permanent neurological injury. He called the neurosurgeon on call and made arrangements for transfer.

"Dr. Callum," the unit clerk called to him. "Dr. Williamson is on the phone."

"Sir," he answered, his respect for his superiors bred from his military training.

"Ryan, I'd like to see you in my office. Is there another physician who can watch your patients?"

"Yes, sir, but I would prefer not to leave right now. We are getting slammed and have already had two major traumas this evening."

"Are there any major traumas not managed at present?"

"No."

"Then I'll see you in my office now. This won't take long and you will still be in the building."

Ryan didn't have time to respond before the other man hung up. He walked up the three flights to the administrative offices, knowing what he would find. Dr. Williamson's receptionist showed him into the office, where Kevin was sitting, looking overly smug.

"You brought this on yourself." He snickered as Ryan took the place beside him.

Ryan balled his hand into a fist and then forced himself to relax. A few minutes later Dr. Williamson entered, looking unimpressed at both men.

"Gentlemen, I can't tell you how much it does not impress me to have to come in on a long weekend to deal with this complaint.

"Dr. Callum, Dr. Dufour has filed a complaint alleging you endangered a patient by refusing to transfer care following a motor vehicle trauma." He paused and looked directly at Kevin. "However, I am well aware that you have more trauma experience and are a better physician than Dr. Dufour will ever be so I thought it would be best to remind him of that in your presence. I trust you two can figure things out from here. Good evening."

Ryan tried hard not to smile as Dr. Williamson left the room.

"You may think you won but that had nothing to do with you. I should have known he wouldn't have been able to be professional."

"Because?" Ryan was waiting, waiting for him to say something about Erin.

"Because he thinks I fathered and abandoned his precious little bastard grandchild. Well, the joke is on him. His perfect little stepdaughter got herself knocked up again, but this time it had nothing to do with me."

"How do you know?"

"Because I had a vasectomy right after the first time she played that card to make sure it never happened again."

"So you are the reason Erin thought she was infertile?" He looked at Kevin and wondered if he had any idea how much pain he had caused the two most important women in Ryan's life, and realized he didn't care. Seconds later Kevin was on the floor, holding his rapidly swelling face with a look of sheer confusion.

Ryan looked over to the door that had just opened and saw Dr. Williamson standing in the entry. "I forgot my briefcase. You should have that looked at, Kevin." And he walked across the room, retrieved the forgotten briefcase and walked out with no further words spoken.

CHAPTER THIRTEEN

ERIN WALKED THROUGH the hospital's front entrance, eager to find Ryan. She knew that he had gotten the same call she had last night, confirming he was Jennie's father. Even though she'd known what the test was going to show she still felt hopeful that it would prove to be the turning point between them.

Her pager went off and she recognized the number of the maternal fetal medicine unit. She had continued to follow Chloe in her pregnancy and had arranged an urgent ultrasound for her that morning. If it was normal, they wouldn't be calling.

"This is Dr. Madden," she announced as her call was picked up.

"Please hold for Dr. Young."

Dr. Young was the perinatologist who was following Chloe in conjunction with Erin. "Erin, I just finished scanning Chloe Darcy. She's just past twenty-six weeks in her pregnancy but the baby has started showing signs of acute heart failure. There is also reverse flow in the umbilical cord. I think you need to get her delivered."

"Thank you. I'm in the building and will be right there."

Erin felt a panic she hadn't felt since her own pregnancy. She couldn't let anything happen to Chloe's baby. Not when she had already gone through so much. She knew that the finding in the umbilical cord meant that a stillbirth could happen at any moment and she had to act quickly.

She ran to the ultrasound unit and directly to Chloe's room. She could tell from the panic on Chloe's face that she had already been told the devastating news. She had to stay professional and do her job. "Chloe, when did you last have anything to eat or drink?"

Chloe knew the reason Erin was asking. She needed another surgery, and urgently. "Last evening," she answered. "The baby's in heart failure," Chloe declared, looking at Erin, obviously hoping she would say something different.

"Yes," Erin confirmed. "I'm sorry, Chloe, but we need to get you delivered."

"I'm not ready. The baby's not ready. I'm only twenty-six and a half weeks.'

"There's no other option, Chloe. The heart failure and the reverse blood flow in the umbilical cord shows that the baby is at high risk for stillbirth at any moment. Dr. Young is reviewing the images and she is on phone to the neonatal intensive care unit now, letting them know what to expect with the baby." She didn't want to scare Chloe any more than she was already scared but she needed her absolute cooperation and time was of the essence.

"Erin, what's going to happen?"

For the first time since entering the room Erin slowed herself and sat down next to Chloe.

"Right now the baby weighs about two and a half pounds, but some of that is swelling from the extra fluid that has built up in the baby's tissues. Following birth, the baby will be intubated for respiratory support and also given some medication down a tube and into its lungs to help the lungs mature and make breathing easier. We can use the umbilical cord to establish intravenous and arterial access so that we can both monitor the baby and provide medication and nutrition in a more direct fashion. There is at least an eighty percent chance of survival and a fifty percent chance of no major complications."

"I haven't exactly been doing great in the luck department this year, Erin."

"Chloe, we need to focus on the positive. We diagnosed the baby before anything really horrible happened and we are going to get you delivered right away."

"A Caesarean section?" Chloe asked.

"Yes. It's the fastest way, and the baby is still breech right now, making a vaginal delivery a poor option."

"Okay," Chloe agreed, and Erin felt a little relief, knowing Chloe was accepting of the plan.

"They are preparing the obstetrics operating room across from the nursery. We need to walk to the unit now and get you admitted so we can deliver this baby as soon as possible."

"Okay."

Erin reached over and grabbed the paper drape, wiping the jelly from Chloe's still-exposed abdomen. She helped her sit up and then walked with her as quickly but as calmly as possible toward the obstetrical unit.

"Chloe, when you get on the unit it is going to be chaotic. Everyone is going to be coming at you, asking you questions, getting you changed, poking and prodding you to get you ready. I have to make a call and get changed into my scrubs. Just remember that you and this baby are going to be okay. Do you have any questions about the plan or the Caesarean?"

"No."

"Chloe, do you want me to call Tate?" Over the previous weeks Chloe had confided in Erin about her relationship with Tate. Erin would never normally interfere in a patient's personal life, but Chloe was her friend and she knew that she would regret not having the father of her baby at her delivery. Erin had.

"Yes."

Once they stepped onto the unit the predicted chaos ensued. Erin squeezed Chloe's hand hard before letting go. She went to change and then quickly made phone calls to Tate and then the blood bank. Chloe's pregnancy had been complicated by blood antibodies she had created after she had received emergency unmatched blood products with her ectopic pregnancy. Now it was even harder to find blood to transfuse her with if she needed it.

She felt her whole body shaking as she watched Chloe being sat up for her spinal anesthetic. The last time she had operated on her she hadn't had time to think about the fact that her friend's life had been in her hands. At this moment she thought she preferred that. She watched as they laid her down. It was time.

She waited until Chloe's abdomen had been painted

with antiseptic and then covered her with surgical drapes. The room continued to fill as the neonatal intensive care team arrived. She found herself looking at the door, praying Tate would get here in time. She couldn't wait for him. Then he arrived and took the spot next to Chloe, where he belonged.

"Chloe, can you feel anything?" Erin asked, as she pinched her stomach hard with a pair of surgical forceps.

"No," Chloe answered.

"Patient is Chloe Darcy. She is having an emergency Caesarean section. She has no allergies. There are two units of blood in the room, and she received a gram of cefazolin at nine thirty-two. Does anyone have any concerns?" the circulating nurse asked, as she completed the presurgical safety pause.

"No," Erin answered, when in her head she had a thousand concerns. Would Chloe's baby be okay? What would she do if Chloe hemorrhaged again?

"You can proceed," the anesthetist confirmed.

She held her hand out for the scalpel and followed the line she had made months earlier. The room quieted and she focused on the technical aspect of her job and not her feelings for Chloe. Within two minutes she had made the uterine incision.

"Uterine incision," the scrub nurse notified the neonatal team.

"Chloe, you are going to feel some pressure on your abdomen as we help get the baby out. Tate, if you want to stand up you can watch your baby being born. The baby is breech, so you are going to see legs and bum first," Erin counseled both parents.

She cut the last layer of the thick muscle as gently as possible so as not to cut the baby. Clear fluid drained into the drapes and onto the floor. Two little feet protruded immediately and pushed against her hand and she found herself smiling, reassured by the little one's spirit. She went through breech maneuvers, being as gentle as possible with the delicate newborn. Once the baby was out she showed Tate that they had a son as the little one let out a small cry that was the best sound Erin could have asked for. She looked briefly at Tate, his eyes glassy as he looked down at Chloe, and Erin smiled, honored to be included in their moment. She handed the baby to her assistant, who took the baby over to the resuscitation team before she continued with her job.

Her sense of reassurance didn't stay with her long as Chloe started to bleed heavily from the uterine incision, the uterus too soft to close off all the blood vessels that had fed it while Chloe had been pregnant.

"Tate, I think I'm going to be sick," Erin heard Chloe mumble.

Erin looked at the blood-pressure monitor and saw that Chloe's pressure had dropped.

"Open and hang the blood," Erin ordered, as she tried to clamp the corners of the incision while massaging the uterus, begging it silently to firm up.

Her actions were in vain as the blood kept coming. She looked at the anesthetist and he understood that they were in trouble with no words spoken.

"We need another four units of packed cells and two of fresh frozen plasma crossed and in the room. Open the postpartum hemorrhage tray and have a hysterectomy tray standing by, please," Erin commanded.

"It's going to take at least an hour to cross her for more blood," the anesthetist responded.

"Then let's get on it," Erin responded, frustrated but knowing it was the truth.

"I'm going to put her out," the anesthetist declared.

"Agreed."

Erin injected the uterus directly with medication, with no effect. She was running out of options. It had been thirty minutes since the baby had been born and they were only getting further behind.

She looked at the hysterectomy tray. She had asked for it to be opened, thinking that if she opened it she would never have to use it. Now it was looking more and more likely that she would have to take out her friend's uterus to save her life. The fragile little two-pound boy that Chloe had just delivered would be her only child and he might not even survive.

She resolved to try one more option then she was going to have to move on, no matter how much she disliked the other option.

"Can I get the B-lynch, please?" She saw the nurse's brows rise beneath her mask as she put the hysterectomy clamp back on the table and instead handed her the elongated suture.

With care Erin sutured a tension suture through and around the uterus until it was physically forced to contract. She watched for two minutes and saw the bleeding was better. She closed the uterine incision and watched again. It was now dry.

"Dry?" she asked her resident, who looked more shocked than she did.

"Dry."

The anesthetist stood up and looked, too, his nod a subtle agreement with her assessment.

She watched and waited for another ten minutes, but there were no signs of further bleeding so she began to close the incision and in twenty minutes Chloe was being wheeled into Recovery. The baby was in serious but stable condition in the neonatal intensive care unit but was already showing good signs.

For the first time since she had been paged, other than the brief moment at delivery, Erin thought of Ryan and Jennie. She hadn't heard from him since he had gotten the results and that both surprised and bothered her. He had already accepted that Jennie was his daughter so she didn't understand why he was holding back now. She glanced at the clock—it was two in the afternoon. She dialed his cell phone and waited—no answer. She tried his pager, only to get the same response. She wanted to find him but she couldn't, not for the next couple of hours until she was sure Chloe was stable.

Her pager went off an hour later and she didn't recognize the number. Hoping it was Ryan, she dialed.

"Dr. Madden, this is Dr. Williamson's assistant, Beverly. Dr. Williamson was hoping you could stop by his office this afternoon."

It was an unusual request. She and Stephen had never interacted personally at work, and he certainly had never had Beverly page her while she was working. Was she in trouble professionally? She checked back in with Chloe before heading to the administrative offices.

"You can go right in, dear," Beverly directed.

Erin still stopped to knock at the door before letting

herself in. Stephen was behind his desk, going through a pile of paperwork on his desk. "Take a seat, Erin."

"Okay." She did as she was told.

"I thought you would want to be the first to know Kevin handed in his resignation this morning."

Of all the things she had prepared herself to hear, that was not one of them.

"Why?" she asked, utterly surprised. Kevin had spent months, years, trying to force her out of Boston General. It made no sense that he would leave now.

"I believe it may have something to do with the black eye he received last night and a lack of support from hospital administration."

"What happened?" Erin was still in shock, and was that a twinkle in Stephen's eyes?

"Officially he walked into a door. Unofficially Ryan Callum from the emergency department gave him what he deserved."

"Ryan hit him?"

"No, he walked into a door. But I have to say I am very fond of Dr. Callum. I hope we will be seeing more of him."

She didn't know how, but Stephen knew about their involvement and she was surprised at how much his approval meant to her.

"Thanks for letting me know." She smiled and excused herself from their meeting.

Erin unlocked the front door of her apartment, anxious to see Jennie. Seeing Chloe's son today had only made her feel more grateful for her healthy child. She walked directly to the living room but Jennie wasn't there. Instead, the entire space was filled with long-stemmed red roses and Ryan. He was dressed in a gray pinstripe suit with a white shirt and matte red tie that matched the single rose he wore on his lapel.

She inhaled sharply, only to have her senses overtaken by the scent of the fresh-cut flowers.

"What is all this?" she asked in confusion.

"What you deserve. I know you like to focus on the meanings of things, your tattoo, Jennie's name, so I thought I would tell you what I need to tell you in every way I possibly could."

"With roses?" she asked hesitantly, her hopes growing by the second.

"With red roses."

"Ryan, do you know what red roses mean?" Oh, how she needed him to say it.

"They mean passionate love, which is how I feel about you."

It wasn't enough that he felt passionate toward her; she knew that from their lovemaking. She needed to know he loved her. "You love me?"

"Very much so, and I'm desperately hoping you love me, too."

"I do," she confessed, her words giving her a sense of freedom.

"Ah, that part I was hoping we would save for later, but if you insist." He reached into his pocket and pulled out the most stunning ring she had ever seen. "Erin Madden, would you do me the great honor of becoming my wife?"

"Yes." And she watched in absolute awe as he slipped the ring on her finger.

"You aren't just doing this because Jennie is your daughter and you want us to be a family?"

"I'm doing this because I love you and there is no other woman in the world I would want to be the mother of my children."

"We just have Jennie." She hoped that would be enough. She remembered the look on Tate's face when he'd seen his son.

"I need to tell you something and I hope it will give you more joy than heartache."

"Okay," she answered, wondering what else there could possibly be.

"I had a conversation with Kevin yesterday."

"A conversation?" she asked, with one eyebrow raised.

"It started as a conversation. He told me he had a vasectomy right after you two were married—that was why you couldn't have more children after your miscarriage."

She felt anger and joy at the same time. Anger for everything Kevin had put her through and joy at the possibilities that had just opened up for her. "We can have more children?" she asked him, as though she didn't know the answer to her own question.

"Yes, we can."

EPILOGUE

"Push—one, two, three, four, five, six, seven, eight, nine and ten. Take a breath."

She exhaled, her breath hot against her damp skin.

She felt the cool cloth being pressed against her forehead and the plastic of the straw against her lips. She took a quick sip of water, trying her best to relax every muscle in her body and not think about what was coming next.

"Okay," Erin managed, and she took the offered hand and squeezed it hard. An incredible pressure overwhelmed her as she tried to focus her efforts.

"You're doing great," Ryan murmured quietly.

As the contraction passed she looked around the room, knowing that any minute her life was going to change. The lights of the delivery room were low and aside from Dr. Thomas and the delivery nurse it was just her and Ryan.

She pushed again, and again with the next contraction. "I can't," she cried out, completely exhausted.

"Yes, you can. You've done it before and you can do it again," Ryan encouraged.

"That was different. Last time I had an epidural."

She tried to argue, but had to stop when another contraction brought on an unbearable urge to push.

"And this time you have me. I know how strong you are and I know you can do this."

She opened her eyes, which had been closed from the pain, and looked at her husband. He was right. Last time she had felt alone despite her mother's presence. Now her life was completely different. Her pregnancy had been a complete time of joy, her fear of losing her baby not a dark cloud lingering over this pregnancy. Each milestone was new again as she got to reexperience it as if it was the first time through Ryan's eyes. She had a husband who loved her and was 100 percent devoted to her, and together they had a happy, healthy four-year-old daughter, who was with her mother in the waiting room, eager to find out if she had a new brother or sister.

"All right," she agreed, as she reached deep inside herself to find strength left she hadn't known she had.

She pushed harder, her focus on meeting their child. And then in an instant her cries were joined by their baby's. She opened her eyes just as she felt their baby being laid on her chest and she reached up to hold the baby against her.

"We have a son," Ryan murmured, bending down to their level. "Thank you for our son. I love you, Erin."

Tears of happiness streamed down her face. It was the moment she had always wanted and finally had.

Two weeks later, their home was filled with laughter and celebration. A baby "sprinkle" Chloe had named it when Erin had tried to dissuade her from hosting a baby shower. But she couldn't disagree with Chloe's argument that she had never had this with her first baby and their family deserved a proper welcome.

"I think he wants his momma," Ryan said, handing her their son. The nine-pound expression of their love snuggled into her arms immediately, recognizing her scent. Already Ian was the spitting image of his father, from his dark hair to the shape of his eyes, there was no doubting whose son he was.

"Did you have trouble picking his name?" Kate asked, her one-year-old daughter, Darcie, bouncing happily on her lap. Darcie, named after Chloe, even had the sense to look like her namesake, the surprising swath of red hair she had been born with sealing her name fate. As neither Kate nor her husband, Matt, had red hair, they had taken it as a divine sign.

"I've delivered enough babies to know what not to pick. Fortunately, Ian did not look like a Dynamite or a Twister so he was lucky there." She laughed.

"Come on," Chloe teased. "Think of the luck he would have had later in life with women with a name like Danger."

"True, it was a tough choice. But we knew we wanted a Scottish name and when we found Ian and learned it had the same meaning as Jennie's name we knew it was perfect. They both mean 'God is gracious.' Ian Madden Callum. My maiden name in honor of my father."

Squeals of delight erupted loudly and all three women turned to look as Jennie ran across the living room, her pants mysteriously gone, with Chloe's three-year-old son, Spencer, chasing her. Spencer, who had been born premature, was still a little on the small side but made up for it completely with his robust personality. He was completely fearless and spent most of his time scaring the life out of Chloe and Tate.

"She does that these days. Most of the time it's funny, except when we're in public," Erin explained, still smiling.

"I still can't believe that it all worked out. If you had asked me five years ago where I would be now, I would never have guessed this," Erin commented.

"I know. It's amazing, isn't it?" Kate agreed.

"It's hard to believe that at one time they all wanted to hit each other," Chloe commented, nodding her head toward the group of men who stood in the kitchen, conversing but also keeping a close eye on the commotion in the connecting family room.

"In Matt's defense he was insanely jealous of Tate." Kate laughed, now able to make light of the complicated path to love she and Matt had taken.

"And Tate didn't make things any easier on him, or Ryan, for that matter," Chloe agreed, knowing her husband and his protective nature.

"But it's all been worth it," Erin agreed, thinking back to the turmoil each of the women had endured on their road to love. "If we hadn't gone through all of that then we wouldn't have all of this."

She looked at Ian, then Ryan, and then at Jennie, who was carefree and happily playing in the family room, and knew she deserved this. They all did.

* * * * *

15_INSHIP2

215_ST_8

MILLS & BOON®

THE ULTIMATE IN ROMANTIC MEDICAL DRAMA

A sneak peek at next month's titles...

In stores from 6th March 2015:

- **Baby Twins to Bind Them** – Carol Marinelli *and*
  The Firefighter to Heal Her Heart – Annie O'Neil

- **Tortured by Her Touch** – Dianne Drake *and*
  It Happened in Vegas – Amy Ruttan

- **The Family She Needs** – Sue MacKay
- **A Father for Poppy** – Abigail Gordon

Available at WHSmith, Tesco, Asda, Eason, Amazon and Apple

Just can't wait?
Buy our books online a month before they hit the shops!
visit www.millsandboon.co.uk

These books are also available in eBook format!

215/03